The JFK Order

by AE Reiff

Grand Canal
FLYWAY BOOKS
2023

Acknowledgments

Grateful acknowledgement to editors where these stories appeared include *After the Pleasure Party, Antipodean SF, Cafe Irreal, Camel Saloon, Dada Yow, elimae, Gone Lawn, Defenestration, Eyeshot, Festival Writer, Frigg, Full of Crow, Futures Trading, Ghoti Mag, Gobbet, Jack, Mannequin Haus, New Dead Families, The Dream People, Orion Headless, Sidebrow, Showbear Family Circus, Smashed Cat, Squawk Back, The Fiction Review, Vulcan: A Literary Dis-allusion, Why Vandalism Journal and Ygdrasil.* "Orcapoi Review" or How the Orc Adopted its Present Name, was recommended by *The Rumpus,* "(in which you will learn both everything and nothing about Orcs) because it made my day better" (Here Я Some Essays I Like). "Overflights from the Desk of Pedro Escadero" and "Herbal Cures of Orc Tongue" were nominated by the editors of *elimae* and *Ghoti Mag* for Pushcart Prizes. "Help in the Steps," was reprinted @ *Fiction Daily.*

Contents

Nabu! Nabu!

*Nabu forms a language isolate unrelated to any other among the Blattaria. Like the Balalabamm or Saurian languages below, it is of unknown origin except in the center of words such as incu**nabu**la, another origin of the Prodicul later developing together with the theme of the Wonk Yap. These hidden documents and similarities, either as an initial prefix of **Nabu**codonosor from which that nation comes, or found on the sacred tablets at Cheese Blocks and in the Mars Writing below, <u>Hamogamous</u> Johnny with other isolates of the New Folk Sensorial Compound express in these languages that absurdism that commerce, religion, and art make unconscious. It is again, another attempt to break through into symbiont mind.*

Nobody Johnny went up to Coalcrotch House.
Brothers from the coal pile down had shot a sisters' spouse.
Ants stormed the rouse, mashed Coalcrotch hopes.
Then came the Call
Hamogamous!
Exterminate them ants!
Nobody made president.

Nobody donned the Top Roach Hat.
Nobody combated wasps.
He placed the old Roach Nabúcodonosor upon his head.

On Blattaria they spoke! From roofs they wrote the
troops!
Fellow Blattopterrans marched with pride.
Nabu! Nabu! they cried.

But this was not the only crux that drove the Coalcrotch out.
Elders prate when a Coalcrotch saw a shoe it should retreat.
Escape by oversight, dodge left or right!
The average shoe gives time!
But Johnny called the plan outworn.
Johnny, "the shoes have grown!"

Those leaders heeded a Coalcrotch brain e'en bigger than their own,
that swarmed a change, then won the prize, high heel in back of the
shoe!
He broke it down to Coalcrotch Town,
"Not left o' right go down!"
A New Day Dawned.

Congress lunched as Johnny told the high place in front of the heel.
Village nymphs enchanted crooned as Johnny the plan revealed,
"no left o' right, go down!"

Congress rose up!
Critical mass!
Here was a roach with theories to match
They passed the law that day and marched them home.

From the kitchen wings they flapped, soared like Coalcrotches from
space,
Johnny saw a Bigfoot then and flew toward the battle place.
Victory to the symbiont!
Johnny made a beautiful move!
Safe in the high place! Johnny! Johnny!
But stop! Look out! The heel! …

Strum Sewer slammed them all that day between the left and right.
El Presidente muert, it said,
Congress assembled like flies.

Koalrathie Lost! The story told how Johnny brought peace for the
roach…
Hurt under his cup dreaming health care passed…
Breaking new ground that silver spade…
Made a sharp thrust in his back!

Johnny dreamed the bill was law and it killed him.
THAT'S ALL!

The Laurel Roach was ready now to sit on a hero's brow.

Strum Sewer led with the front page news on the stoop beside the towel.
In the bathtub then where the funeral was held for the Nabu leaders who died,
rolls of Coalcrotch jammed them in, *Ho foen! Hoe fen!* They cried.

Many a Thatched Oothecan hung on the humid wall.
A Coalcrotch in Black came forward and spoke:

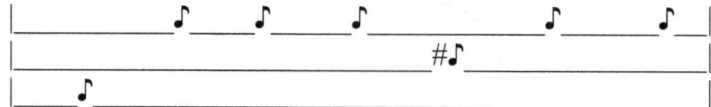

♪ Fellow Coalkrotchians we come,
to honor in behalf,
Remembering with willingness,
to praise him in his death.
Let each one now perform his part,
and sing in praise of Johnny' s heart,
And take… this… step… to
welcome our Johnny home. ♪

Three Big OOps

   *When the auction clerk in Hong Kong rang up a complete set of the books of insects of Coleoptera it challenged that whole set of assumptions that divided the phyla from each other; insect or mammal I can't make up my mind. Offered by Gorham with pictures in color of each known then of Hybrid Etymologies of OOps from the early berms back to the postHomerica of Pyrmonidies wasn't it. These analogies back to when they had fiefdom of assembly in physics and Matter were useful to contain the taxonomic classes, the same as protesters on streets of various phyla were anything but human, but more idea in their hybrid natures. All these attested to those updates in The three Pillars of **O**bject-**O**riented **P**rogramming*

*(OOP) as encapsulation, inheritance, and polymorphism, in the
picture writing of long heads before.*

Once upon a time there were three big OOps who lived in the town
of Dubity. Turk OOp was the father, Mom OOp was the mother, and
SueLit baby looked like her dad. The OOps were fond of a bowl of
sausage in morning with ginger snaps stuck in the side. They were
quiet OOps if you didn't count the chickens or the occasional
gaseous emissions.

Mom belched at Turk about his 800 pounds when he and Sue OOp
walked in the park. Their footprints filled with water and drowned
little dogs, the first sign. Mama defended little dogs in spite of the
proverbial puppote they would cause. The Pups eat off Dame's floor,
which has plenty, since she ate, as all OOps do, galore.

The second sign of OOp is passion. Ma OOp, or Dame Belcher,
sometimes called Guapa Pop, has many names. She is also known as
Grizzie OOp. It's a figure of speech.

When we say that Dame Belcher read Sue OOp and her dad, that
book is a conglomerate for what Turk published about Sue OOp as
both purveyor of Pop and its publisher, who lived in a gingerbread
house with smoke coming out the top. So here we have an 800
pound OOp and a fubsy 600 pound OOplet. When he retired from
publishing Turk wrote his own book and married OOk Mama amour.

So what do you eat when you eat SueLit, a broadside big as a ham?
Clerihew oeuvres, poems entire, anthologized stew? If it's the cure
that ails ya, drink milk in your poem. Sleep aid, hunger? Roast
PupPoetem in your home. Sue Lit is a beauty cure!

What doesn't Sue Lit cure? She's a grape of the huge alone. With a
piece of the bone then the world would be one! One peace, one
world, one home!

Dame longed for something to eat. The sense is elastic. She had
other books too besides the PupPoets, who lived in the back of her
Olds, a Schnauzer, a Pomeranian, and a Pifawa paper. Little dog

PupPoets longed to read as an OOk. Turk published these too, but the thought goats attached to Dame's bumper were the ones who blabbed. So huddle up for breakfast. Lunch pasties will be served with Ham on Rye. Dinner on the left and a modem on the right. That's our Sue! Where has she gone? That's what we're here to show.

Guapa Susan

Two features come along the mystical and practical cow trail, 1) that it is black and white, meaning simple, a primary attribute, and 2) that it is a place where memory cannot recall any of the changeable things that are done. There is a third implicit feature to the herd in the overlord, according to the ancient. Thus the order of the cow and anti- cow involve mediums of control too many to name. A wake up to something big houses have for entertainment at their Bohemian sites, the names of cows that go missing are not on milk cartons. When an investigation ensues a panel, a commission is appointed. What they do conclude they never do. That is pied cow too.

The neighborhoods south of McDowell are eating Susan tonight.
This is no joke.
Would you like a nice moo cow coming in your yard? With all the trimmings? Susan was as big as a cow and that likened her.
It was logical.
She worked nights and came home in the day. Her car vented smoke like a blue volcano. She put the pedal down and erupted from a distance.
At dawn you looked out your window for the fire. Chickens stirred their stripes. Voices ran like sirens. Crowds gathered on walks. Widows did business in directions. But the fire engines never came.
Susan drove in the midst. Arms waved. Voices greeted her glowing. Dust settled. It was Tuesday. That's what routine will do. The neighbors were watching her. You'd have done different?
The fence rows of that house surrounded Susan. She could still live in a building like you or me. Some modifications had been made,

doors widened, foundations reinforced. Her chair was a two-story bed. One wall sagged in the corner of the floor. The little red phone was dinging. The phone was dinging. The goats were gossiping. You ate Susan and think this an exaggeration?

Science has long proven that the homogenous ecoplasm called earth affects everything else.

So?

Allegory, dude.

Susan lived where no white person should have dared, shorted down to the nubbin, parceled out by the bone!

They saw her largess and loved her, mountain and plain. Word went home.

Come to Susan's!

Kindreds gathered. She pulled to the curb in her red car smoking to appreciative murmurs.

Peepo storked and Lydia cried.

Men in potato sacks around 7-11's tramped out of their boxes for the view.

The Dame of Guapa Pop

There was a basement in their adobe. It was a cold room. When Dame and Susan came over and sat on the berm, they became mythogema. We call them Guapo, Guapa, Damer, or Damer, Turk and Sue. Moon gatherers, indicas of light saw the black and white. Anthropologists from Cambridge west danced Susan with her cowgregants among the trees

Her name was Myth.
Her pop was Guapo Myth.
In his life as Turk Musselman he was an all night party poop along the Scottsdale border.
Susan looked like him, but she had hair.
Sidewalks cracked when they stood together.
Depressions left by their feet in the park drowned little dogs.

Nobody connected Pop's disappearance with Dame Belcher's purchase of a walk-in freeze. Presumption credits that the Dame, Turk's second spouse, had too much brew the night that Myth got shanked and smoked. That was three full years before Susan entered the same.

For all they were nice folks. Goats populated piles of debris.
For all they were quiet folks, never a loud noise unless you count the chickens or the occasional gaseous emission.
The belches anyway were pleasant, made you think you lived on the coast off Hoboken where ferries and tugboats echoed by night.

In this world, home from the bowling leagues, came Sue. She rented balls and shoes. Crowds gathered. Men pinched women and shook hands. Traffic beeped for blocks.

Sue Myth had had the front seat of her car removed so she could drive from the back. Not that she was tall. She was wide. Blocks on the pedals enabled her to pump them up and down.

What are you waiting for me to tell, that Step Dame ate the Musselmons?
This is no joke, but odious as all decay that stops a hole to keep the wind away. Women doing what men have all along, a sign of the time, quartering purple mountains, packaging fruited plains?

There's an excuse for eating Susan? The profit of developers? Who pays the taxes, gets permits? Neighborhoods are zoned for cannibalism?

Smoke poured from the gingerbread chimney.

She ate Pop.
She ate Sue.
What are you waiting for me to say?
Him and her? That's all there is.

It's a case of provocation and murder.
One day she was there. The next day she's gone.

>"She's gone, she's gone, when thou knowest this
>thou knowest the swell carcass Sue Myth is."

2.

Sue Myth went her way o'er hill and dale, in wagon and under arm
to the Frigidaires and stewpots of the Danger Mountains.

The dark moon of January,
cool breezes of light,
porch slivers were quiet,
Susan had not been seen in weeks.
Chickens were silent as canal ditches.
The homeless drifted home.
Dame Fortune wrote on the canvas of unmaking.
Freezer humped a blues.
Sixty Watt tramped out the back of Belcher's hutch. That sissy bulb
was smashed. Hedgerows ran unbelieving. They came in through the
bathroom window.

Shout, cuidado!

You'd think the glass would tinkle a warning, but it was new safety
glass, no louder in breaking than fir trees that put their feet in
plywood sheets last summer.
How many came is anybody's guess.
A syndicate is implied for the body to spread so far.
Wagons and bicycles if not trucks and trains backed up.

What did the bandits do when they came to that massive barred door,
the freezer room running off the entry?
Look out! Look out!
Go fast, room to room, poke closets and open the cold door?
Sides of beef, chickens hung from hooks?

Or was it packed in white, labeled by compartment like Glendale
housewife, roast under veil, loin in the defroster, and veal?

You only see it dimly.
Freezer light's not bright.
You best see it quickly.
No place linger winter nights.
Quick hands roust the white packs.
Up on boxes, down the hooks!
Fat sausages or arms?
What hams?
Dread Gorgon!

Susan of the smoke and a cloudy day! Susan who stood the walk and
could have been a ghost of hundreds who never dreamed their
expectations this-a-way. *Guapa Susan*.

Relays boost to pickups.
Wholesale all the day.
Others rush to grandma's house.
Slam girlfriend's fridge.
Bang Susan in ice chest.
Sneak her in Mom's Westinghouse,
wrapped as a decorator might.
White paper covered the deed of the Dame, who called police for the
missing, freezer empty, her bead collection on the floor that night.

3.

Patrolmen filled out the case card, took figures for insurance.
Next day, Detective Dave Cash came, with nothing left to do, peace
broken out. That night's initiative? Step Dame let him in.
No warrant was needed to investigate a crime.
Living room led to dining, dining room to kitchen, en passant to
freezer, solid eight by ten.
Officer hesitated entry.
"They took all your meat?"

"Yes, they did! My daughter's missing and I can't find my plates!"
"Have you filed a missing person report?"
"No sir, she's gone! After all the trouble I took in getting her right!
What can I do now?"
"Well, Ma'am, you can file a missing person report and if she
doesn"t turn up in thirty days we can give her to the FBI."
"No, no! She's not missing like that! She's gone!"

The officer advised Step Dame of her rights. Alarm spread our city.
An APB for meat.
Freezers were sought by mothers seeking Susan.
The purveyors thought it a joke.

Weathermen puzzled the news:

"What goes east and west
and north and south
but never stays the same?"

Children riddled at bus stops:

"One, two, three, four
Who's behind the white door?"

It was the eighth wonder of the world in a town that had a spa.

Eating ISue

*We were there when the freeway was built, had moved into
that derelict neighborhood a year before. All social relations
fragmented, leaving behind drug houses, gangs and illegals. Our
immediate six neighbors on all sides were women widowed white, in
their 70's, left over from the lowering tide. They had pomegranates
and grapefruit trees and oleanders in which to hide.*

There is a highway right round earth that divides the ley lines north and south. This Gateway tells how one night the neighborhoods began eating ISue. But Susan is not just a problem of dissolution. Our question deals less with her than the road to her and the plight and aspirations of her sister cows, for many distinguished betters have had their Susans. My search led to the memorial abattoirs of her acquaintance. Susan flowed like milk without impediment of mind. A growing body believes flesh wiser than mind. She comes out of a trance trotting home with gladness, a perfect devotion and symbol of good mindlessness.

This pastoral distinction can be understood in the light of nature. What went on in the back yard may be disapproved but not surprised. Driven to pasture and strange excess Susan had the impatience of a duck, the sensitivity of a cat and the nerves of Europe, with Asia and America rolled up, properly speaking, Lady Ottoline, Lady Cynthia and Horrible Dorothy, for Susan was an inevitable result of the discontent of these refugees, suitable among the coal pits of night miners, those primitive Methodists, whose Unknowable nights have forgotten all their bones. Only the one thing to do they did it, invented a private religion which stands naked for the fire to go through, rather an awful feeling, the Beyond with the Unknown that in more suitable times might make us novelists. In this vast impulse Susan waves on like rain falling back again into the sea, a theory of relation and mindless primitive that believes. She doesn't even know me, gloated knowledge. She doesn't know I am a gentleman on two feet.

Why should we even try to know a symbolical cow, approach in levity readers so solemn at her service? As Herr Nietzsche said,

> *Ursula, the teat,*
> *Frieda beyond deep*
> *Gudrun centers squeamish.*

As far as the relation between Turk and his paramour, witnesses reported those lovers heads, feet cups and saucers flew. Tender and unknowable the lumbar ganglion, sacral and cervical, the hypogastric and eightfold polarities.

The Oedipus couple, he was Sigmund the Wagnerite, she a Polish governess. Her favorite month was May. Polarities winging their giddy flights to the dark core of the sun among pantheists and vitalists taking sunbaths, carrots and squash of a new Wordsworth sitting on his cold grey stone would assemble on platters, the daisies Plato were positive. Cups of peppermint, dark promiscuous pairs of the very female sort had a soothing effect when they sit, heads in their sides, milking they are solaced. As Susan milked they gazed into her eyes, which tragedy in every cow has been both comedy along the sylvan way.

Cows of peace and plenty.
Cows and pines, drum and dance,
If Susan had gone to her nest among the trees that night
she would not have wandered west.

Susan might wander in the moon the adept of sleep. Cow and moon are known from that pineal daughter of the Chaldee who sees Susan plain in Atlantis moonings. Not just for the mindless and the primitive express this discontent.

Susan in Swedenborg was an early name for cow. Syntheses O Altitudo, starved by Darwin, had Susan nude before the Flood, those happy to exhume her passing.

These bridge the Birkeland gap between myth and land. From Bolivia to Moscow metempsycowis was the experience of these disclosures. But cows don't eat at night.

Shall we dream of equal love for men, women, flower, cow? and their symbolic breasts who made the world safe? My quest of Susan through the depths of animism and mindlessness, though puzzling and unprofitable questions confound the bovolatrous man who could not welcome those explorations of the limits of thought. For when the imagination has failed its alchemy and the absurd raw material remains raw and absurd, the meaning and value of the work seem foolish in devotion to the actual cow. The world as bad as the confessor allows, broken under, tore from the roots that clutch, closing barren leaves, the plight of sensitive men

That Bergson and Nietzsche fled with reasonable men called to Wagner and his congregants. The deep of Wagner called to social and economic orders to find a cow, not merely the cow of the flesh, nor merely the lost cow of youth, but a strong and wise cow of the mind's life.

The great Fred Nietz thought us all happy cows whose rivulets dance in beauty born of murmuring sound. Cow poets, that cute little donkey a mule or a poet? Believe it not we could answer this. Do you wonder why they looked for fire when Susan drove up in their midst and waved? Fire is the spark extinguished by sky in cold air. Were they proud that Mercury had crossed both angles of the county lane.

Cow speech reverts that tongue prospecting spades and boots. To say there is some ethic prime directive of electrosmog, something like phantasia -inversion, or as said about Silent Weapons for Quiet Wars- "found in an IBM copier at a surplus sale," suspiciously dovetails with the lost Borges years, that shoot situations, instead of bullets.

 As the thinking moon came nearer to SueQ, it gave text to language rays. Project "Silent Talk" detects the word-specific neurals before speech to see if patterns generalize. Wide Eyed-- Persistent Stares of drone use mosaic video and auto-track pattern-of-life data from cellphone cameras inside the footage area, chronograph movements and forensic rewinds of footage catch the Gorgon Google Stare.

But to leave this primitive plumbing for you spiritual creatures who see beyond Marie Antoinette and her milk pails croons, it was in Phoenix we met Susan upon the berm, Susan who ate pumpkins to so much success. Susan out nation among the dances. Susan of the cows, fore the timeless symbolic breast of ages. Look reverent now you triple sized Mack trucks on interstates.

Lit and Und On Shunt

I could have sworn after Grapefruit class when I read in Baudelaire's "The Martyr," that "the head.../ On the night table, like a ranunculus, / Rests," that this, as promised in the ranunculus in our garden was where the "golden crocus / fills the cup / of ox law / and ranunculus." Maybe an alternate version read, "the names are changed to protect the ranunculus." But there it was right in the middle of the page: "Our neighborhood holds the garden principle." These legends of the Acéphale of Bataille are mere Swiftian Professors in the remains on Shunt. Bataille never dreamed the decapitation of Louis XVI as a joke, and promising to venerate, just like the New Borns of Old Oley did, Nietzsche, Freud, Sade, along with discussions of sacrifice so *woderful to intellectuals of the absurd that alternate herbals morphed plants as disembodied heads.

The Argument

UndPrint on the inland border
was an enforcer, had a gun.
SueQ looked like him, but she had hair.
Sidewalks cracked where they stood together.
Depressions of their feet in the park drowned little dogs.
None connected UndPrint's disappearance
With Damer's purchase of a walk-in freeze.
Presumption credits that the Dame,
UndPrint's second spouse,
had too much brew the night
that Und was shanked and smoked.

To put it plainly, things were going well until the murder.

Call it what you will when Lit and Und were killed.

Damer showed artistic taste to want them as an hors d'oeuvre, a
delicate preserve.
Yes, frozen they would have stayed, so some part to this day would
remain.

But when the freezer broke...well, that's too discreet.
It was broken into, pillaged, its remains dispersed over town.

We are not talking just literal meat.
Dragons want the good, not food, gold and all the blood wherein the
body is preserved.

Two levels occur.
One physical and literal, with murder, meat and thieves.
The other, where murder by carnal appetite is more like allegory.
Once murdered, pandering I guess to lower nature,
boors, literary swells and the personal, the corpse was et, whatever.

First remains were parceled out on shunt, the web.
Multiplied by thinning, increased in space and time,
even with gruel the dragon could survive.
Concepts seem to fail.
The End.

***

Here's the tale.

Dementis Dramatis Personae:

UndPrint: The Behemoth of New York, LA, DC elite.
Guapa Sue Lit: His daughter, art and the nation Innocent.
The Shunt is Inter-et.
Damer is carnal appetite.
The freezer holds bicephalids.
The park is Mother English.
The little dogs, perverts.

***

In the publishing industry of New York, UND or UndPrint, known as Halfling Talk, sometimes Turk for his weakness, would walk the park with that equally obese progeny and protégé LIT. There is a family resemblance.

Guape (a) was her name, not in the Latin, but in the Saxon, gape or galp, "pando (j)aepe."
We call her Guapa Sue.
Und and Lit, or Talk and Gape together, have many names. They can be OOps or Ooks.
Their massive size made huge BICEPHALIC IMPRINTS in the park.

This PARK is language where their footprints swamp and swell, endangering nouns for food which here refer to prey.

The imprints made by Und and IT fill with water and drown little dogs.

These dogs are the Puppets who did not belong to LIT, but even so followed Und, their greatest enemy that endangered them.

If lost little dogs make us sad, when we compare them with what happened to Halfling and his Dirk, taking cue from their referents in Und and Gape, we confront our ultimate fear.

UndPrint's second wife was the befallen appetite and its carnal embodiment.
They used to call them blems.
She was the awesome DAME who could be called a dragon of appetite,
though you might think her merely government.
She kept the house of Und and IT, but slaughtered them and stored the first remains.

Appetite's sides fall in where you stand.
Dragon strikes endanger many lives.

Why do people stand on shores and look at skies?
Why stare at monitors, image in a glass?
Appet-pit is apposite of inward search.
The beaches, benches are crowded there.

But to make the matter short, both LIT and Und were consumed,
even though they nurtured and made hungry appetite itself.
This is quite unfair, to quote the bane who said, they are made.

Add to these referents of Und, LIT, and Dame, the SHUNT, for all
too soon Sue was parceled out with Print, the thigh bone severed
from the knee when Damer's freeze broke in.

Allegory spells it out. Daily UndPrint and darling LIT
may look like chickens hung from hooks, but not.
Quick hands on boxes down the hooks, but this is no sausage, ham
of Gorgon.

For that more was left of Gape than Talk for Turk was taken full
three years before.
Und and Lit were broadband soon on Shunt.
You see this means more late nights, electricity, people thinking they
know it all as dragons reproduce.

Exhumed to this inland border, the Shunt-conveyed remains of these
behemoths were kept like mastodons in ice.
This at first glance was right.
Science is based on theft.
The dung of 10,000 years is more important than you thought.
You think that's funny but it's not.
If all that's left of the past is dung and bone,
how important is iT for our next world when the victims are frozen
in Dame's home?

Which made it all more devastating when they were stolen.

Damer thought she could live off them for years,
gave no thought to dinner when they were gone.

Recycle dragons where you can!
This cavernous lack of planning implies appetite might not survive.

E pubs on Shunt remained, combined both torsos into one,
distributed as inter-et their own.

This was the Dame's last sustenance.
Ironically, Und Halfling Talk was a precursor of this Darjeeling
shunt.
It is called Darjeeling for that global pressure point.

The remains of Und and LIT on Shunt recombined in the torsos of
Talk and Gape were called Êgenerate.

Recombinant genera of fish and cow we know.
What should we call this? Chowder, stew?

Dame's recombinant carnal appetite consumed Shunt's recombined
craze:
closed loops, solipsists and their troops, that is, the frozen remains.
To give it its due.

We should have inquired of Talk's first spouse and wife,
because that Dame was his second.
Whether she married before Halfling Talk is uncertain.
She was second but was he her first?
We want to get Gape's mother in on this but the answers are myth.

We backtrack to what Und was, which tips it.
It's a typo. Und was Un. So Und first married Un and begot IT.

Could it really be two beginnings produce another shunt?
Carnal appetite always wants good eats.
What did it eat before LIT steaks?
Lit survived three years from New York 's demise,
then was burgled.
Had Halfling Talk been appetizer enough we'd not have had to have
Suelit on Shunt.

Clearly, carnal appetite knows no bounds.
Itself contracted myth, was maw consumed.
That's how Hrothgar ate and was eaten, but that was before Shunt's war.
Now the Dame, in remote control, can be triggered from afar,
not that that is better than the rest, remember to say it together:

<blockquote>
carnal appetite,
carnal appetite,
carnal appetite
has taken the very best.
</blockquote>

Political allegory abides religion.
Damer cannibalizing LIT, supplants men who had been doing it
as many intimated, but it's hardly our job to decide.
We mirror only what we see. The rest is left behind.

The Key

These plot wrinkled, home burgled, frozen remains parceled over
town have given moderns pause before the fridge.

Is that allegory or what?
In social science Levi Strauss built an urban myth with the effrontery
to ascribe ourself.

But all myths don't look like Fafnir.
He was promoted dragon from being dwarf, so he bettered himself.
Nobody compares him to Puff or Damer.
All-knowing dragons are pretty rare. True knowledge is closer to
ignorance.
We all know that.

Giants are a lot less knowing though, and you can certainly count
father and daughter among those.
But to who else but Fafnir can we go to think about the unthinkable
consumed?

Dragons and giants essentially lead to this, that our ideas are
basically worthless and we are devouring ourselves as we speak.

In myth's supposed picture, archetype the reverse, what's thought is
true.
If you think the false is true, true false and the opposite of real is
real,
 like in movies, fiction, life is fairy tale.

That it is before your eyes at all is to the curious and dedicated
history of these times just a footnote.

Concepts of the Subfornical

*The ocean and forest of that rooted world of winters and
epidemics of the original Massachusetts Bay or Botany Bay,
adjusted by the errand of the Uberman, speaks to the subfornical
necessities of this POPulation. The bicephalic fingertips of
Ubermensch and a new worldliness of enemy in the ordinary hid the
uncanny in the everyday. Fantastical forms in the familiar couched a
trap of peasant revelry, grotesque dreamworlds of the everyday of
cosmic hostility. From the beginning gluttons, misers, quacks and
libertines were replaced by ravenous superman, the literary
Breugels of new worldliness.*

I have done what anthropologists wanted, taken back the native as
my own.
It admits too much to live the other way.
Whether at bus stop or back fence where these stories pass as found,
plain speaking without fiction embarrasses the text.

Away with your Eskimo and Caribbean divines, myths carried all
along.
Excavate the Caucasoid within! You will find that primitive thought
lost in forests of homeless scutter with those wandering scutes,

troglodytes of leather whose shells scupper an alternate universe.
Folktales there were performed at banquets in large quantities.

You cannot mistake the OOk-Ork Planet.
Bent to either side for vertical retraction, OOk-Ork pops straight up
like a prairie dog in its burrow, then **goes globular.**

When rotation tongue replaced AngleFrank as OOk-Ork's best
weapon, a kind of mandibular debasement, an octopus with tentacles
furiously spurting ink occurred.

The irony of this is that antidiuresis and reabsorption of ink back into
the terrestrial orifice caused opposites. The cartilaginous attachments
of OOk-Ork being more complex than either amphibian from which
it formed, tragedy mounted it at just such a time it was least able to
sustain. Of reptilian turtle orders, twenty two subsumed to four

Talk about open conflict in podernum man!

A carapace surrounded the subdermal.
Whether reptile or bird, OOk-Ork's thespian ancestor argued a
fusion of jaw and mandibular arch.

This mandible constructed as a lower jaw, a cranium, displaced in
truth from the brain. Examples are not commonly encountered.

The Hox code of OOk-Ork speech affected the upper lip with
pharyngular twists.
Its anomaly impacted skull structures and jaw formations.
Division into oral and literal dissociates at the skull base made it
exaggerate. Orthognathous vs. prognathous jaw: Morganucodon, the
Lamprey.
If you open OOK-Ork up you find an everglade.

The Wonk Yap Is Coming.

Fish groggy with plume, dark within, that flourish and pump out the mastermind, drawn on a scale three or four times as large in the middle, the little people who worked there, if such can be said without profiling, were not from anywhere exactly. Slabs stuck up out of the ocean into which they had driven the krill, being a little larger than you would expect, which made that celebrated bagoong. After the original 79, the majority north of the equator, 116 are not on the first maps, in either the dark regions or the light.

The Wonk Yap is coming.
Shopping carts circle fires on access roads, cooking meat, villages built up over years. I took a look at the excess driftwood. The neighbors wouldn't talk. It was up to me.
I burgled their houses while foraging.

Wonk Yap will downfall *Homo sap*, take women underground.
People on waterways realize this. They infiltrate into yards.

There are Wonks in hidden documents, similarities.
They are named.
But people don't want discussion. Government knows and is afraid.

You see analogies. Draw your own conclusions.
The common name of *Homo wonk* is itself a pun. In the city called a wild *gyak*, it is a *wap* in country homes. The cook can be a wild wok.
That's easy.

This beast resembles *Homo sap*, but *Homo yak* you've heard, has two legs, breeds in open places, is hairy. Research nears completion.
Even considering its inner nurture it is not a clone.

This Yap has affronted many. Detectors at home centers are being wonkufacted by the beasts themselves. When you see it, if you want to ask when it began, read on.

They beast's within, but within where we'd like to know. Ask the
Atavist.

If they differ from our neighbors they differ from our friends it
would be fatal to mistake from either end. There aren't many
choices, either a Yap is bestial or we are one ourselves.

Neighbors do not deny that monsters with gills and horny heads steal
children along the canals. Project Canal does not deny this was
revealed, and that does explain the acid burns on arms.

 Citizens want to know, should we go down to the canal and defend
our homes?

But humanitarians argue we should take the Wonk Yap view. How
does it feel to their youth in combat to be lied to, told by superiors
"oh, it's just a bruise," when a .22 long rifle exits below?

Psychologists reconstruct our dreams with fears, ask us to
understand that the sea man in us is us and we them.

What happens, when shot in the neck, stolen child beside, acid
glands moldering, generals send innocents to their demise? Or are
we men?

People have ignored the signs, slime on the banks, troughs where
webbed feet climbed.
They ignore the dreams.

 Do not argue the lists that the Yap is making. Many rumors occur in
the Wonk Yap taking. These appear in the unguarded talk we here
attempt to forestall.

 We have made a chorus, go around and sing, "The Wonking Yap."
It's that urgent to break through to mass mind. Is that confessing?

We could go around naming. You're a Yap! You're a Yap! It's hard
to be wrong. Somebody's one! Many urge we give addresses, license

plates. Which one is this, this one and this? Alas that I was born for such a time.

I'm not saying that we should give the beast a chance. I'm saying we should take our country back. Yap math teaches that the parts unequal to the whole. Yap literature teaches that less is more. Easily turned, these attempts are self defined. Is your experience of more, more, or is it less? To Yap promises don't you just bawl? That's already on cereal packages you say.

Is he him or us? Does it sound like your boss or your brother? That's the problem! How can anyone know?

To dispel these rumors we probed the beast's poetry, the primitive in waiting. But the wonk is skillful in disguise. He uses protective coloring. He talks like a Democrat. He talks like a plebiscite. There's a Wonk Yap in history and math, that's plain, a fundamental Wonk feeling.

They don't go to school. They swim the ocean for krill, are found in libraries and buildings.

Yap aspirants don't creep on their bellies in slime, they are not what mother brought home from grocery, all teddy and fluff. Yaps practice, indoctrinate their young to be like us.

Where no man has gone, where blood pounds the fish groggy with plume, dark within, Wonk flourishes, plans and pumps out its mastermind.

He thinks he's perfect. Why else would he want your wife? Why does he live in your yard? *Veni vidi vinci*, or in other words, "me man, me."

If a guy is acting bestially is he a Yap acting humanely? Somebody from Billings wrote in to ask about his dad. "How do I know if the shrunken head my dad got in Ecuador in the 30's isn't the head of a monkey?" That is our problem.

Have you never suspected an entire cow was buried beneath one skull in a garden? I went for proof, shot my pencil down. It was as soft as peanut butter to the top. Even if bones are elusive, something will turn up.

To what lengths these creatures go to preserve themselves! The Yap is burrowing, insinuating, sneaking. Has it got a soul? Can it be saved? To these burning questions what answers can give?

Homo sap must decide while Yape is creeping whether to reach down and engage him in dialogue like Tolstoy or drive him out into the waste, assuming at this late date we cannot eradicate the manster.

Thinking wonkishly may defeat him. Think wonk! Hardly is that wack out when an image troubles my site. Have you seen it, diabolical and cunning, sly and self serving, does it sound like someone you know?

Is your local grammarian a Yak? Will civilization be overturned by taxi drivers, journalists, teachers? Pity the child clutched by a Yape. Eek!

Yaps will vanguard homogenization, remove difference of ambiguity.
Yes, yes, yes, and no, to all the above.

Wonk is smarter than believed. It can regulate air. Breathe now, but the Yap meter is running. If they will not wonk, let them not breathe!

Yak wokery! Woeful popery! The Wookeries are teeming yet not fully grown. Their cabalists push down to the pet shop to liberate one. Will you? If so they have won.

Do you approve Yaps umpiring the Major Leagues?

Government computers theorize that hybrid forms making other forms prove that the thing that looks like a thing is another thing and not the thing we think. Writers have spoken of wong yaps and longsocks, begets of wog and bobbleys, of bogaries, facquis, lopi rotisseries and wacquiries! An egg will look like a gibbous moon.

If it looks one and talks like one and acts like one how do you know it ain't?

Herbal Cures of Orc Tongue

These Orders of Causation & Response (ORC) were early ThoughtGoattens that passed into gas at Ghoti without notice. They had been nominated for a Pop Tart! That has "'changed of course now that the Orc has achieved ascendency in world culture, transcending nationality'" (The Rumpus, 2011).

Western Orc first started its predacious colonies in sandpits along rivers lined with horsetail reeds. These *equisetum*, a wide-creeping perennially jointed variety, were a remedy for bedwetting and STDs. Orcs would ply the hollow reed between the joints. The gritty silex was also used in Orc scour, the ritual shaming of captives where victims of the scalding tongues placed in Orc pits were flayed with polluted reeds, slagged until even the Orcs themselves could hardly swallow. *Orcapoi* lived with constant sickness, ear ache, irritability, and cough from these habits, which had internal consequences as well. Orc is no Korzybski. Its loose speech of a braggadocio nature, using words as loose as its bowels, was a malodor equal to the LaTourette syndrome of its writing which prevented further atrocity however since Orcs are prone to inaction. In an Institute treatise, *Orcopolis*, the Virginian showed psychiatric acculturates of Orc domes simulate social freefall. Tours of the domes have rekindled inquiry.

Orc tastes a lot like turtle so Indians ate it raw. The Hopi applied its essence for vomit and Orc water was a laxative. Mrs. Niebuhr believes that the whites of East Texas ate it. But what did Indians eat so much of they either had to throw it back up or need a laxative for? Orc! Once thought to undress at night and remove the outer shell, detached Orc should be seasoned with croton in the edible part between the cracks.

You may be standing on some croton right now. It looks like a maypole round which the faeries of middle earth might dance. They took it as a tea before the settlers drove them out. Eroded soils make a vacuum for Orc. Fertilized by the Spanish King, a Squamish Bug that plows gullies into seedbeds, croton fragrance revives the natural. When Indians no more hunted and no one else could stand it, the horehound Caucasoids combined with Orc predation and Orc lore passed. Orcs went openly undisguised as inhabitants.

Treatment of the Orc malaise first began with *Zanthoxylum Clava-Herculis* when victims sat to pass their verbal habits. Lumping real and unreal together, carrot and hemlock, vitex and cannabis, ilex and pyracanthas, defense against this malaise was promoted by the *Zanthoxylum* "Hercules Club" of raised nodules which formed a spike in the hand of anyone collecting Orc. *Zanthoxylum* camphor protected speech. Insert it in the mouth of Orcs before gagging. A leaf on the tongue will soon make it numb. If you don't gag Orc it will seriously vent. Many affected Orc paradigms benefit from this. Companion half Orcs who mime Orc talk shut the mouth and are freed.

When the Orc sought the extirpation and extinction of all natural and social worlds the humble Cement plant began its detox in stem and leaf. *Concretus perspectivist,* especially the *particularis* ground, was dehallucinogenic and cured Orc tongue. Discrimination of true and false emerged. Pharmacopeias gave *Dessicata minima* for too much drinking and rhubarb for too much sex. Where on the path to Erebus aren't branches of *pavlovia* and ephedra good for failing Orc, vexed and bored Orc, soul sick and drunk Orc? Combined decoctions of Purge-Sweat also relaxed the surfeit of Orc neglect. Then they forget the dust home they are buried in and are made of as well.

Salvia was an enemy of this putrefaction long before Orc. Even when suppressed by accommodation politics it was a main defense that "God will help you." But Orc imports supplanted it with a foreign *divinorum* domesticated in homes from the wild that gave futuristic properties to the foreign. Half believed it could foretell while the other half believed it protected from what was left, a society of excess treasured in the one hallucinogen. Real species were thus substituted by this shame of the hot house. Gardeners took its inebriation even when the catlike odor produced disturbed visions of their neighbors.

But *Salvia regla,* a low growing symbiont of hummingbirds and doves, drove the Orc out. Ruby-throats swarmed the anti-aesthete so that the Orc could not abide either in the lower limestone nor the higher granite altitudes where *reglas* flourished, for large hummingbirds of those altitudes prospected the two meter high shrub. Apple green ovate leaves truncate its base topped by candle flames five centimeters long. Dark green above, glabrous, hirsute and glandular beneath, racemes of scarlet corollas hid in canyons and on slopes atop mountains. Chased by that hummer of high mountain Orcs fled to sandpits in the cement range and further retreated, encountering their ultimate nemesis, the potent desert creosote, *Larrea tridentata.* Orc-cleansing not only in sand, but on the rock and hardpan that underlay, that flesh preserver implied a spiritual cleansing too, with *hedeoma* and *monarda.* Cement from the crustaceous lac upon the branches at long last compromised the Orc carapace. Vast creosote colonies of interrelated roots prevented Orc not only in air after rains, but on the ground and under.

Its intellectual and emotional capacities degenerated to the physical, the rough skinned, claw hand Orc clashed on the rocks of its own paranoia and inner dislocation. These fused realities became symbolic. Whether the living tongue of Anglo-Franco-German Orcs augers a global Orc plied from the debasement of the American. Language goes to the heart of the dying culture that Tollerson previewed when he said that Orc transformation begins with the shedding of the outer shell.

Sources

Carroll Abbott. *Texas Orc Newsletter.* Kerrville, Texas. 1976-1980.
Henry Burlage. *Index of the Plants of Texas.* Austin, 1968.

Gary Fleming. *A Guide to Plants with Edible Value.* Austin, 1975.
Gorrell and Hobston. *The Orcs of Texas.*Renner. Texas Foundation, 1980.
Brother Daniel Lynch. Orcton *Plants..* St. Edward's University, 1974.
Alta Dodds Niebuhr. *Herbs of Nearby Areas.* Austin, 1977.
Odeffers Virginian. Moscow Orc. The Separatist Institute, 2002.
AE Reiff. *Native Texans: Philosophic Contexts.* Austin,1984.
Reports of the Experimental Drug Garden, College of Pharmacy.
P. Tollerson. *Conundrum in the Codonts.* Glasgow: 2000-2007.

The Armors of Ummim

One of the terms "I will found you in sapphires" is that the Council of the community in the assembly of their elect like a sapphire in the midst will make the battlements gems like the sun in all its light and at all gates glittering stones. That there's a fragment and then the text breaks.

Naked they chanted their hymns before the fire in front of the standing shields. We'd not know any of this were true if not for the survival of bone from the undersides. These heated and cracked by the Amerind fashion of the ancient Chinese reveal that in the far past it could remove the shell.

If you've never bucked on a flak jacket when you want to take it off, which feels like a tourniquet, the security of this bulk changes when there's a desire to go naked. Orcopoi wanted safety but the shield bound their life, which took a curious relief in remedy, if you've a liking for disparate facts. It grew a kidney as a third brain to alleviate the pressure. That and the ingestion of silicone reeds which provoked diuresis regulated the body in the plastron through cycles of desiccation and uresis. This required a whole new way of life when they permanently removed the shell. Living in utter nakedness was of course another problem.

Burrowing along waterways, its predacious colonies interpopulated sandpits where it loved to stretch in the sand and rub those reclusive parts with reeds. This first caused the diuretic property that is our concern, I mean the principle by which it escaped its own imprisonment.

There are three stages. At one point the shell cracked. Ancient Chinese used a pin to create the oracle bone script, but Orocopi had an organic crackling of the shell interpreted as the same. The vagary of these oracles led it to prey upon other species, fragments of which serve as oracle bones today, art forms interpreted in the craquelure of shell. These have semantic import beyond decoration. Indeed it formed colonies of a higher level of culture and began to hunt others due to its own predation.

A conflict in the archeology and anthropology finds that these creatures survived even the late settling of the West they once ranged, moved back up in the mountains where they were more intelligent than first thought. Archeology, anthropology, politics, and finally psychology became legitimate expertise. For all that these the shells were the best informant.

A shield is spherical and covers the midsection and chest. It attaches over the shoulders and down the back. In that sense it is a carapace. Once detached or detachable, over the course of survival it maintained the shields under stress until they literally fused with the scute, the dermal bone beneath.

The shell of this scute has a thin ventral plastron whose epidermis is a leathery skin, but the scutes and dermal bones do not have the same composition, which explains the craquelure. Fine networks of cracks occur when the shell shrinks and becomes brittle. Craquelure also records the environmental conditions the shell experienced as an exoskeleton.

The jet black carapace matures to a deep amber under the extended prognathous jaw. Even if an insect derivative, the pantheon of diversity claims all phyla as relative. Genomes connect to the claw that protrudes from its helmet in stress.

The celebrated and imitated patina produces a pattern of hairlike cracks in the varnish of mature shells. These apparent floral patterns, whether from UV light, shrinkage or age, appear in the armors of the Smithsonian. An Acanthus baroque styling older than Rome marks early hand hammered hardware in its rosemaling. Whether the result of natural force, or manipulated at will, this craquelure throbs with wide sprouts or barbs. Fissures reverse to forks, especially when there are ribs in the pattern. Inscrutable crack formations of simple branching describe neural networks under black light. Dimpled fingerprints, fine cracks in the finish, cleavage, cupping, spirals and dimpling occur.

The aesthetic appeal of these chest plates compares with ancient Greek Vase painting, even more because it is a force of nature that so decorates it. To what degree that being cooperates individually in the making of these designs is debated. The relation of shield is personal and intimate, meant as a mask to frighten enemies and inspire the imagination of friends, so it is no extreme to say that it is its personality is a shield.

The shields together tell a communal story, decipherable as words and paragraphs out of their large storybook. Their wars and their gods are Norse in effect. If this seems foreign to designs produced by nature, let it be compared with the fossil record that tells a grand epic even as geology shapes land. How these natural forces interact on personhood in the shields, making them figurative and narrative, is our study.

J. J. Tollcork

Mule song, grizzly bear, Leo, coyote, Johnny cake,
Squisquatch, Nabu, oropoi, cry of goat, help in steps, pancake,
anthropology of orc, pity, the wonk yap, "within minutes of turning
patients with low oxygen saturation on their stomachs, they saw
oxygen saturation levels jump back into the normal range. "Patients
who were coming in with oxygen stats in the 70s ... once we proned
them, after about a few minutes, they'd be up in the low 90s,"
Various explanations of Orc genesis occur, Cain's wife not a
daughter of Adam, his children's imperfect descendants
interbreeding to produce an antediluvian Orc, or a cerebral
hypertrophy-induced ideation of power over nature so great it
became the ruling class.

Tollcork's misinformation included spinal adjustments of remedial
wing sockets. The Hollywood Orc thought and said a lot of things
foolishly believed, but we should not think the Orc false even if
its intellectual and emotional capacities degenerated to physical
characteristics, a kind of LaTourette's syndrome in verse. The
jagged fangs, yellow mouths, red tongues and eyes just show the
Orc's debased habits. Tollcork tried to prove it had been tortured
into Orcness by savage alien interrogation, as though Orcs were
from space. They were cannibals true, if understood metaphysically.
The Tork school had them in foul pits and tunnels prejudicially
slavering, spawning and rendering a cartoon of poison darts and
scimitars. There is no room here to explore the clash of Orc armies
even if we grant its subservience to the MoDork wars surviving. The
Orc escaped and sought peace abroad where it continued
fighting, serving buffalo and wolf on a piecemeal basis, but not so
prolific in breeding, its territorial imperative gone. It became a rough
skinned and claw handed back yard breeder, lost heinous trappings
and lived in communities such as you still see in Arkansas.

Orc writing reflects Orc speaking, itself a surprise, being of bird
origin, ostrich or egret, articulating from the epiglottis out the beak.
Stops occur in the back and front of mouth due to the odd shaped
tubular jaw with side tunnels digesting flesh. The Orc voice is

subdued with these pockets full, but empty they echo, which roaring enables its seduction of prey. The shoulder sockets now fleshed over show where wings once attached. The Orc is above the ape but beneath the dolphin in this. Blick first mentions that Eternity shuddered when they saw,

Orc beget its likeness,
On its own divided image,

but Blick did not have the benefit of modern research. Further confusing, the inveterate Tollcork, took it to Hollywood. Even Tolk himself used the words *og* and *ob* before designating Orc. It all depends on whether we believe it a foreign presence in that ancient passage.

The bestial significance of its evolutionary reptilian likeness to old myths of half men half beasts was only secondarily like the bestial case of giants. The monstrous includes a deeper depravity than thought, a hyperspace Orc, a marooned arthropod degraded from citizenship, a debased angel coming out a bug. Orc paranoia differed in its ability to solve epistemological questions of destiny. Inner dislocation and personality dissolution fused those separate realities with the monstrous.

Orcs never properly understood natural law and force, arrogated privilege from the breast. Breastfed an inordinate time, Orcs deactivated the coping mechanism of survival. Present the teat what need respect nature?

Science does not credit that the Orc is real. Whether it is medieval allegory, simply the worst kind of human being, we would like to forget. A third opinion suggests we share traits with it even though it has debased itself. Orc mind or heart as our own is a recession to fantasy. We hope in future to arm public defense against such defilement.

Orcapoi Review

*I couldn't get fiction out any other way. Editors took to
calling it essays. "Is this more of your meta-ficton," I was then
asked, as if I had just returned from travels to 18th century Spain,
where four tongues resembling AngleFrank, a Mandibular pop
defibrillate ink that spurted everywhere when OOk-Ork popped
straight up, whether were everywhere.*

To explore the beast, the first mention of Orc was hardly hundreds of
years ago. It had a quasi noble birth and place, eventually debased.
Early insight in "repressed love turned to war," resulted in the
confession that Orc "stole thy light & it became fire consuming"
(*Four Zoas*, xi, 147f). An entire hemograph on this is justified.

Orcish ways, Orcish talk behemoth in its boasts got play in science
fiction as an intermediary race of beings who lived in dark caves as
brutes that plundered at night. It doesn't need genius to know how
these came into being. You cannot escape symbol even if you put it
to death. Toss the coin again on top the maxims then scrape off.
What's beneath retells Aeschylus, Grimm, or Mabinog from first
likeness to the last consumed, discovering in consciousness what one
would never want to know.

Astronaut-anthropologists plummet the depths to overlook the
backgrounds of our world in theirs, undiscovered what they cloned.
This natural and spiritual parallels our own. A mythless people shorn
of symbol so much that they must do to others what was done to
them in order to disbelieve their own fear attracts squatters to break
apart the self. One might say having eaten their effigies of disbelief
they could not judge who should retain life and who not.

**All that has changed of course now that the Orc has achieved
ascendency in world culture, transcending nationality.** It
represents a series of attitudes and prerogatives that dare to define a
new reality utterly different from that ordinary one of caves and
holes and black blood. Orc has gone global, and while it looks like a

man is no more a man, as classically defined, than it ever was. Please allow us to forego saying exactly what is a man.

Orc thought is never at a loss for words so while it may refer to mythical races or the Scarecrow of Oz, or an Ork that acts like a flying horse, and a dozen acronyms like Origin Recognition Complex of DNA code, none of these prepare us for the truly extraordinary excitation of its flaming. Change the appearance and you change the life.

Flaming

In a Scienficic Examination of Orcs a thing can be more than one thing at the same time it is two, so orcs as orcacles of the high and the mighty are also low down, creatures of habit and appetite akin to those you might know, not that any of your friends are, understand, but maybe a little. There has been a trade in orc skeletons which seems as good a time as any to admit to the discourse on invisibility had yesterday with one who argued that if invisible he would just feel around until he found it out. Well put, master, if your one sense is all you lose to blindness and not them all, for then they would all desert you and disappear.

That this is literal will of course be denied. Taunts of spontaneous combustion will be heard. The bounds of science are hardly ever believed, especially in such reclusive and secretive beings. When the moment of its taking off approaches, Orc withdraws from what was a very active outer existence and goes into hiding in the most remote place it can find, the deserts of south Texas, huge stretches of Nevada, any number of national parks in off season, especially Grand Canyon. I say this is hardly believed first because there is little evidence after the fact that combustion has occurred, as would be natural in an explosion, since no damage is done. The effect is taken as heat lightning, and secondly, since it happens often at night, there have been few if any sightings outside anecdotal folklore accounts. These as we know can hardly constitute evidence, like anecdotes of Sasquatch and Loch Ness.

What solid evidence we have comes from the Orc itself that in combustion its flaming occurs only after it feels compelled by nature and its own confinement to divest the (outer) shield. This carapace is a subject in itself, but the method of taking off is germane. Partly because Orc is such an extreme being, given to moods and mood swings, its extreme rhetoric being proof of this, it had an on again off again relation to its shield. At one point the shield was organic like a crustaceans, but various frictions created inner drives to be free, for the Orc will be free of all constraint, that is its mantra. The frictions were from mutation too perhaps, and better diet played a part when Orc grew enormous and had to shed the shell or be crushed within.

The ingenious manner of this taking off has been celebrated, I mean its desiccation, but the result was that the minute Orc was free of the shell it sought to be bound again and manufactured new shields to carry on its primitive forays, that is before these were sublimated into the offensive rhetoric it now possesses. That this was done serially further complicates so that at no point in the evolution of the shelless state can it be said that its evolution is complete. Sections of Orc geography seem to undergo this separately, which argues that it may after all have a viral cause, that the loss of the shell is a kind of live Orc decline, leaving some untouched but affecting the whole with disastrous results. On again off again, the shells became the best record of the Orc. Lost or buried and dug up they gave account much like the hieroglyphs of Egypt. All this is beside the point of Orc flaming except it shows the background of some of those studies that have consumed the orcopologists of literature. The flaming thus has been inferred to occur from further compromise of the skeletal structure after taking off the shields. Simple sunlight, UV rays, oxidation, wear and tear away the exostructure. Even under the clothes that the Orc wears in modern times this occurs as an inevitable product of entropy. When one goes missing in the modern, missing person reports notwithstanding, but only in Orc circles, and these are closely guarded, is it understood that a final rite of passage has occurred. As noted, many disappearances attributed to crime could easily be explained this way. Suffice it that erosions of outer being contribute to the explosion.

Superstition Benefits

*Late in 2007 <u>Kanzius</u> RF Therapy claimed that <u>radio</u>
<u>frequency</u> <u>transmitters</u> can also be used to generate a hydrogen-
oxygen mixture dissociated from the <u>memory</u> to make <u>salt water</u>
fresh. Water burns was another. Water with a memory affected by
cell phones was the discovery the EcoPods traced initially to the
work of Poe, set according to Earth's axis to activate simultaneous
hydrogen fusion in each second of latitude and longitude per
quadrant. This was microscopically done to ensure even and
gradient combustion for all. "Burning the water" it was called."*

E. Pluribus Unum downed his glass with a snoot. The whitened pate
of that bald head shone like the dome of the Federal Building before
demise of the old order. The claw of his hand that had bent to many
a coed instruction now swept the air to the tune of *Sapless Foliage*,
an esoteric quartet wearing octopus suits and tennis shoes.

These musicians endeared themselves to our company, playing the
Order of Response and Causation, a fusion of country hymns with
lyrics based on the Declaration of Interdependence, the occasion
being another glorious 4th, that gala event when the august removal
of evil from our nation, state and world came to pass, *anno dominus*.

"Is this not the best of all possible worlds?" The Old Burgundians
celebrated with their mundane cousins. If ever souls were driven to
exactitude, here the least denominator lay in conventions of the
intellectual sort.

"Phoneme and form my brothers: the syntax-drive of the Telus
pyramid is sound-fired, sound-fused and sound itself."

Sir Farther spoke:

"Achilles dragged Hector thrice round the stones boys.
Shall we who sit upon his shoulders, do less?"

Thereupon he produced a rubber mass, connected it to a freon air horn, as did others at the table. They proceeded to blow up life size versions of the Trojan shepherd. Each horn attached to a bellows to disembogue that learning of puffs. They blew up their dolls in unison. It was an afflatus of the ruling *seculorum*. Then with a hoot, these numbered in that advance shuttled thrice around the table dragging their Hectors and singing

yo ho, yo, ho, yo ho.

This sensation was in tune with other events of the evening where gents in frog suits pummeled each other singing *Et Tu Brute*. A tall string bean of a man who made *eructions like a volcano hung from the ceiling. Producing a mask like a giant fig, he escaped via a trapdoor beneath to shinny down the fixtures, landing seat first in the pudding. All their philosophy was delivered with such oracular eructation. Declaring " above and below," eloquence of sacred effluviums affixed to their temples with catch bladders, happy epithets of *turgidus* and *inflatus* issued from emitting and receiving organs.

That chief fountain head descried, "there's more in these patties than tofu!" Members of the Druggists' Association had lost all control. They leapt chair to chair chasing a buxom girl dressed as a pill dispenser.

These were the merry causes that passed the bounds of *umwelt* among us who celebrated the world free of evil. Absurd and glorious under the new rule of *Anything Goes*, the old system of *License* was transformed in the new *Liberty* as our druggists let off steam from repressed ages of duplicity.

E. Pluribus knew that with his glass of milk he drank equality, society and brotherhood, for the Pied Cow was now also an accepted citizen of that new order to "leap about, eat, rest, digest, leap about again, morn till night and day to day, neither melancholy nor bored so that when asked, 'why do you not speak to your happiness but only stand and gaze?' Then that cow would answer, "I forget what I was going to say."

Without evil the innocuous blossomed to that grand state known to us as the Each-All.

Homogeneity was all in each and each in all, not separate, but homogenous particles in the cosmic pattern.

Peace bloomed in new harmonies on cola cans, subliminally linked to reduce tensions by their packaging. Sodas were also spiked with the druggists' latest discovery, Happy Peace, a trank that was a euphoriant too. This operated metabolically needing only periodic boosters, endemic, since everybody drank it like water. To be safe the water was treated.

The past polluted All-Chem was now a breakeven synthesis married to exponential life style, for pure water gives pure effects to everyone favoring pure chemistry.

Colonial beef was available for all, for cows were now bigger than garages, self contained meat packing houses, and better fed too upon the treated effluent that fertilized both cabbage patch and lotus root, everyone's favorite.

The new housing bubbles needed no roofs. There were neither roofs nor window cleaning, for the *Enginactory Organism* breathed with the environment and was easily inflated at no cost, just like the prophylactics distributed in high schools at the end of the old era.

A perfect transaction obtained in the earth community. *Ecoponics*, the water-based freedom for all, rehearsed evil into oblivion. The *EcoPods* set Earth's axis to activate simultaneous hydrogen combustion in each second per quadrant, ensuring even and gradient combustion for all. "Burning the water" it was called.
Each person furthered the means of existence, true openness to social conditioning. Peace, peace, we cried in our youth and now peace ruled. Up and down the chain of duty and response, society functioned like a universal child.

Did Sir Paddington know he drank equanimity with his milk? Did Sir Farther know? How can a pioneer of great cities with universes founded upon his effort know the full effect of all he has done?

I say to you citizen, is this not the best, the most perfect of all the worlds?

Invisible Giants

The gills curve up to meet the stalk, notched to join the top. Whoever's on the ladder then swaps their cow for a wonder stick, a bee that sings and a fiddle that plays pop-tunes. Puppoets love pop tunes where that good cow Milky White with all these wonders appears in the tales. Climb the beanstalk, cut it down, exchange a cow for seeds that grow to climb to the gates of heaven, Jack Bommb, that moonlight regular found his way to this Bazooka Temple that serves all those who climb the sky.

Once when the Giants of Family Und roamed canyons and ballooning heads, there were giants of Rhine gold too, in opera and children's books. You'd think them clouds till beanstalks sprout from their beds.

If giants better knew their work they'd not eat those who fed them as their food. Tidy one mess, clean up stuff, tie the bibs when they throw up, after a hot meal the company of little dogs comes in.

Kept by giants, but consumed at times like candy bits. grown from stock which their minions possess, it all comes down to the Mouthful Feeding Anomaly of these little pets. PupPoets they are called, but the more they eat the bigger giants get, which breeds more pasty imprints of the whole.

A jolly giant is boisterous in its binding, but small acts of compression occur when privileged Professors broker deals between giants and the little tykes. The aim of course is to make the giants visible. This however causes sanitation problems if it distracts from the cleanup of stumps and littered dens.

PupPoets cannot say what's not and at the same time clean up what is.

Do giants want to appear or not? PupPoets follow the imprints to the stalk where they chant the not, and squirm in its direction to make giants show by gravitation.

PupPoets would catch giants in a net like wind, but these Encephalites are invisible as craters on the moon. Wherever there's a hole PupPoets produce a slump to cast the crater impact of these "footstumps." *O cognentis solipsis*! You may think there's nothing at all when PupPoets sound the metaverse.

In time we analyze this sonar void perforce, how it breeds, what diet, how the roughage of writers keeps it balanced, which amazes us only when we know.

Sky giants on earth and PupPoets are not the only fits.

Hydrocephalic obesities are pastured on innumerable farms of readers in town where giants force their chickens and cows, readers and thinkers of the day, as we do herds.

In feedlot libraries and slaughterhouse universities the mind is after all the flesh the monoploid eats.

Sure it makes a lot of talking, but as they say in slogans on buildings in town, "Prospect the Mind." The better cuts of Professor Yum are there. Each discipline grows more food. Religious schools and Industry enlarge the dole. Eight billion today, eleven billion tomorrow, giants multiply fast but need more silo. The food base grows too slow.

Measuring population by the feedlot first, we plead for better crops.
Giants from other planets have been assigned a need to colonize.
No food is greater than this need.

Lemon Platt on Fairy Tale

We came to Phoenix for the internship, ended up next door to Ken Morrison, in Religion at ASU and down the street from Lew Alquist, in Art at ASU. There were three professors on that block if you count the sometime poet. Ken was a gardener who inspired two stories, Christmas City and Gardens and Grapefruits.

Once our neighborhood sold like lemon platt on fairy tale it came time to pick.
When the grapefruit turned unusual colors our block went on alert. We drew
straws. Assigned to watch a moo cow guy named Ken I can reveal no more. The
names are changed to protect the innocent.

All our neighbors were professors. Art, religion and poetry cohabited one half block. We didn't have scientists so I tried to fill the bill, gave aloe to botanists but ruined experiments. I'm scared of ruining them all.

Ken was a professor of religion caught in a lie about his vegetables. You'd think it venial, that the tomatoes aren't hurt. But if he fibs about the garden what else hides under the surface?

Over the years we had a friendly competition.
He nicknamed his garden Jack Perk.
I ordered email lilies from Jorge Borg.

Argued out of lima trees, he planted *Ricinus* vine.
Had you been in his kitchen, kibitzed in the breezeway, you'd know.
He gave me a *Bauhinia*. I give him the benefit of the doubt.

It is a diatomaceous earth.

Our neighborhood holds to the garden principle:

> Where golden crocus fills the cup,
> the ox will eat ranunculus.

Looking out the window now I see butterflies flutter his *manganate.
Maybe it's a sulfate.
But what are the brown spots and tags on the citrus?
Why does the *aqua vitae* look weather proof?
I should have been suspicious, but I thought it was the mulch.

The choices are simple enough.

Be exposed to vagrants rafting the canals by night or kids lingering at bus stops,
Mariachi music at three AM, where the neighbors clean their yards up once a month,
or ice cream trucks that play Beethoven's Fifth when the Gold Convention comes.

It ain't Holland.

If you think the choices are better further out, fine, go ahead, move.
We're stuck here with pizza delivery. We live in the cannabidiol zone.

At one time our mayor, the governor and the sheriff all blamed the siege of Hezekiah on Babylonian hordes.
But this is America not the Andes!
You're safe unless there's digging in the yard.

Neighbors took to warning strangers when animals disappeared:
"Professor Yum'll eat cha," they said, but nobody hears.

Local forensics came and did a stage two check.
They searched for footprints in soil overturned near walls.
They checked indigenes and indigents that left these clues:

1. Is the incidence of street people down? Little changes in ozone tip this off.

2. Are door to door salesmen and itinerants down? What do they know we don't?

3. Look out, they said, for labyrinth dogs walking backward, stray limbs on the ground, people drinking irrigation water, grapefruits turning brown.

Anything out of norm really, city workers who dig the same street over and over again.

Finally we came to realize the problem.
Yum was eating his students.
They went in, but none came out.

Our teenager argued this was constitutionally protected,
that it was an eating disorder at which we should wink.

He brought out chaos theory, the genetically predisposed,
said the victims were willing accomplices.

For the sake of science I installed see-through curtains the better so
to see.

You can take it as a reference if there are problems in your town.
Is there a lot of barbecuing? Consider what is known.

J. D. Salinger is a good example.

That's his real name you know!
This grad visited his prof at home.

You ever visit your prof at home?
For dinner!
It hurts to eat alone.

I saw J. D. coming down the street ominously named for body parts, for feet, turning down the drive. He parked over by the neighbors so as not to call attention, hedged up against the curb.

Pretty soon lanky characters began to appear in socks.
Where's it safe to live at in these days of spare parts, Kidney Lane?

Great mounds of earth were being moved, pitched in the alley and carted off.
There must be eating by the planet load.
But what's under the surface?

One night when he was at dinner I went over to see, took core samples, ran my pencil down the soil, smooth as peanut butter to the top.
Gas chromatographs are now being done on the lemons.
Something will turn up.

The suspense was great, then I finally went over and asked. He didn't deny it,
said he'd done a chapter on the Abenaki, cannibal giants with hearts of ice
that live at the bottom of Grand Canyon. If you want you can get a copy.

Streets of Christmas

But at the start Ken declared that he would not put up Christmas lights.

I looked over the back fence and saw them playing bridge.
"It's Christmas," I shouted, "there's card tables, they're playing bridge!"

We decided to move in.
One neighbor offered a fresh turkey.
She paid my son $700 to mow the lawn.
He charged $300 to rake the leaves.

I planted nut trees.

A preacher came by Sundays to wash the windows.
I haven't stained my doors yet, but can you blame the neighbors?

I do have questions.
What will Alma think when she learns I moved?
Will she forgive me for provoking the Liquor Board?

Sure there's rumors of pot and gays, somebody planting oleander, so
and so has a girlfriend. Oh it's a godsend!

What do we see on the streets of Christmas?
Morning walkers on the canals, a little old lady with the red chow,
hierophants with scented cigars, and now and then fathers and
mothers.

 Our street opens with bells and prayer, runs to a Christian school
indwelt by doves.
In this ecology I have not seen a bug.

Pecan, citrus, Aleppos yes, upstanding aloes with a green beard, a
diverse race of raven, grebe, swan.

Those who were worst enemies in the old world have been forgiven
in the new.
They play bridge.

Christmas is inclusive of the planets too, with the exception of old
earth, fumigated for the astrologer idols.

Sorry about that.

One neighbor raised a memorial to evil, impaled a passion flower on
a vine trellis.
That got him in trouble with the Association which forbids the
idolatry of past lives.

Our good neighbor policy winked at it.

Forgiving and forgiving proves we are not the little green men the
clipping on my desk said we were.

You can go on and on about Christmas.
But why bother?
I say just live it.

Here are some glimpses of the city.
All spiritual evils overcome by the one good.
Angels chanting rise in antiphonal motion, wings at rest,

"I in my Savior am happy and blest,"

Little choruses flap around.

The bass section is going, "thank you, thank you," always thinking
of another reason for praise and then when exhausted they think of
Him Himself.

Then the tenors come in and they're going, "thank you, thank you."

I tell you getting up in the morning is no chore here because there's
no night.

It feels so good at the base of my brain that I'm going "thank you,
thank you."

It's Christmas!
And Thanksgiving!
It's Easter! And Pentecost!
This is Christmas City.

You have to adapt to all the lights.
There are so many lights it never really gets dark.
They put lights on the trees.
They put lights on their dogs!
I saw a neon cocker, a luminescent cow!
Women in Christmas City have every strand of hair lit with color
coordinated haloes, shimmering sheaths.

Can you imagine the electric bill?

One or two recalcitrants won't put up lights.
I would think they get a rebate.

Heavenly air, chill mornings, pleasant afternoons.
Snowbirds like crazy.
Tinges of cedar.
You can live in town, or further out among the elk.
Did you know there are elk in Christmas?
They spell the angels on trumpet each hour on the half.

Then the coyotes horn in and dogs are barking so that what with the
bird chatter, it's enough, sometimes it's too much to hear the sound
of a baby's rattle.

"There are babies in Christmas?"
It's getting to be fun you say.

"Are there wives too?"
Yum, huh?

Well, there need to be some surprises.
"Good air, good food, good living. Wow! How can I get there?"

Trip to the Heavenlies

1. Understand the nature of the parables.
2. Understand the purpose of parables.
3. See the parable in its proper context.

Sittin' in my car one day mindin' my own business I get this call
from Joe see who says, "the way is now open, the way is now clear
for you to enter the heavenlies."
It was 11 A.M.

"Enter or exist," he said.

How can I go?

"Listen to me" he said.

"Okay," I said, "but can I have a day to think it over?"

"No," he said, "it's now or never."

So I got out my old Rust-Oleum can, cinched down an extra and eased into this phone booth.

"Joe," I said, "are you goin' too?"

But he looked at me with that spaniel gaze, slammed the phone door and before I knew it we were in the heavenlies.

The next thing I saw was the bottom of shoes bowing down to a bust of the Igod.

On the bust was a slot where after licking they punched in their cards.
Then they would go down in a swoon.

I said, "if that's all there is, I'm for goin' back."

But he gave me my own card and led me up to the idol, which I then saw was alive in a sort of way because ooze was drooling out the corners of its mouth.

The ooze filled irrigation channels which connected by tubes to the prone mantises.

Joe got out his card then, licked it and fell down dead.

I was dumb-found, but the idol spoke: "Stick it to me," it said.

So I got out my Rust-Oleum and sprayed it in the head.

Oil and water don't mix, we all know that, but I was not prepared when the ears fell off.

The tongue slid out the mouth and little trees took root from the nostrils into mid-air.

Withal there was a hammering sound so I gave another squirt and the whole thing fell backwards and turned black.

Joe woke, took one look and said, "we better get outa here."

So we got back in the phone booth and here I am.

Ican say it's a fun place to visit but I don't know if you should want to stay.

Palooka Temple

On the edge of a lake in high season, "Exploring the "divine partnership," a lot of dream time wandering in warehouses of the 'New Apostolic Roundtable,' the road signs changed to geometric symbols as I biked by a woman who had a fluffy, red, blue, green yellow bird on her shoulder. It was playful and liked to flip around.

but I did not go down the road, but found an apartment where large dogs were kept and

After my first trip folks wanted me back in the heavenlies.
Joe called, "the way is now open, the way is now clear."
That gaze got me again.
Sudden we were in the phone booth, whooshed up the sky and whomped down into heaven. When the door opened the sign said, *Palooka Temple.*

Joe took out his card, stuck it in the idol's head and fell down dead. I reached in my belt for a can of paint. The Igod said, "no, no, not again," but Joe got up and pulled a lever on the side on the side of

head. Wheels went around real fast and matched up with little dolls.
Bags started filling with cash.

The dolls could talk, but were stuffed.
They were dropping quarters.
Card tables with sweet meat spread out among the neighbors, which
is what Joe said in his *Heavenly Tour* right after, "one way to heaven
unless you hire a rocket."

Joe had a perfect car that could never break.
He was revving his engine next to the bags of cash.
Boy would I like a car like that.
The dolls had cars too, shifting on their cushions.
Just at the thought of this social revolution Joe took off.

Hightailing after him but without a car, I never got a glimpse till late
that night when he and his wife were bathing their Lexus in a hot
tub.
The car was right in there with them.
He had the phone booth in the back.
Mounds of flesh snorkeled over suds and air pipes gorged.

There was writing over the tub.
"Do you know what it is called when you cannot see your feet?"

I took a guess, "fat?"
But the sign flickered off and on.
"Sin!"
"Oh!"
"The fat leaves but the sin remains behind."

The thing had its own commentary.

Rats scurried along the edge of the tub.
In the guidebook it explained, "the number of gold rats is according
to the number of Philistine towns."

Averting my gaze again I lost Joe again until Christmas when the
Igod rode down dressed as Tannenbaum, which after sucking in your
belly all year must have felt good. It was a holiday so we were
honored with a speech:

"To emphasize the past, I am Tannenbaum, not my socks.
I love you as mutton.
I love you with Tannenbaum before, though we do not speak.
Have you seen me on TV?
I am Tannenbaum to you who breathe and I will mention you if you
give me a boat."

I hadn't seen any water.

"Look at this grass," it said, "all Christmas and frosty.
That is your patch of yes.
It is a reward for all the gold tumors Philistia is sending."

I was trying to get back in the phone booth still stuck in his car so I
could make it home.
It's easier to get in the heavenlies than out.

Joe was promising buildings, buses, a college with a birthday
offering and TV when he slowed down for another pick up.
 I took a running dive, just cleared the back of the phone booth and
landed hard.

Somebody shouted, "A donkey's head for 80 shekels of silver!"

Wee Person

*I read this far but then our pal Eagin got a rigmarole about
some allegory of the up and down where Pedro Escadero's kiss of
canyon and sky that peeps jump into the canyon to feel and Jack
Bommb's penlight from above to below, and the tourists that get off
the late night Harvey bus are supposed to show the intrusion of the
whole above/below thingmabob.*

When the
world assembled
and pelvises rolled away
the questions of printers
interrogated each new day.
Clinicians garbed in cubicles
put on pure underwear,
a hundred million
woke folk
flushed emissions in the atmosphere.

Photo cells turned red
lights on.
The sun
Stabbed
Arms
In a
P
U
R
P
L
E
gown,

waving fingers and just rolled up the sky. The illusion began.

Eagin O'Arthur rose with a pit, a hard doubt, an indigestible fear in his finely tuned but erratic brain. Did he know he was now meat to go in the machine with its sensational detail?

The firemen were ready, had been since 1912. The hospitalists with their gating, salvationists as well. Cab drivers and administrants told sums to the counter tops, leucoplasts in their hummers put a bounce in the collective hop. There was no gleam in the collective eye. They were ready to do their job.

Eagin O'Flannigan Arthur, out of the bog by green turf of shamrocks, who had known servants in the Guinness Company, aye, had himself risen to American heights and was unemployed, put on towel racks he did in the accepted tradition and was thought a Jew by the proprietors of lumber yards. A fighting man who at one time had cut English grammar, sliced a comma with discrimination, he went into his shop.

Meanwhile the town of Pied Cow spread itself over sand sometimes buried three feet beneath cemented culverts. It was a dream town with a pool and a spa and a delightsome mayor. Under the sand the fossils of brushes awaited discovery. On top, on top of the sand was dirt. On top of the dirt was grass. On top of the grass was bird seed ready for birds to gorge while cats shirked in bushes, stuffed as they were with yesterday's Cow-Can, the cow in the can that was an horse's hind.

***

Also at this time there was a wee person who was small. Wee person, for that was his name, did not know he lived in the town of Pied Cow, didn't know Eagin Finnigan O'Arthur Flannigan was his father, or that he was to have a social security number. Then the milk blew up.

First the grass was green and the sandpile was filling, then boom, boom, the air was fire and the world disappeared. It was mineral spirits his father cleaned from white paint on a brush. O'Flannigan, Wee Person under his arm, called on the heavenly agencies, the miracle workers of that century, the people who truly made Guinness, the very people so employed. He called for water, Eagin O'Flannigan, oh he called for balm: now save me, he pealed like a bell, ringing and ringing. He was desperate for saving.

Fire trucks came, ambulances. Eight beardless white men in t-shirts stood on the lawn. The grass suffered terribly, the grass was fire. The air was choking. They said, let's go to heaven, and the boggy pool that had formed in his gut flowed to their truck.

"What's his name?"
"Wee."
"What's his first name?"
The fireman served to the ambulance man. Their questions
volleyed him back and forth.

"What's your name?"
"What's your name?
"Are you the dad?"
"Are you the dad?"
"What's your address?"
"What's your address?"
"Do you have insurance?"
"Do you have insurance?"
"Do you want to go to County, State, Mountain Valley, or Goodbye
Samaritan? We can't leave you sitting in our car."

The truck circled. Wee Person wheezed. The building of heaven
zoomed whitely in the rear view mirror. O'Flannigan went inside.
The halls gleamed. Oh the beautiful shine. Wee Person choked.
Attendants with towels and basins ran to catch the spittle from his
chin before it hit the floor. The administration frowned.

O'Flannigan, his red shirt soaked with the oil of his misery, eyes
wide, grasping the equally wet Wee Person, faced off with the
whitened attendants, They stepped back. The apparition spoke.

"Is this Emergency?"
The tension broke.
"Yes, this way."

He eventually came to an amphitheater of white. Machines blinked.
Chairs rolled around the room looking for customers.

"The angel will be right with you, but first, what's his name? Are
you the dad? What's your address? Do you have insurance?"

The hospital clerk drove the ambulance driver into his backcourt. An overhead smash placed in the backhand corner. Then he punched the ambulance driver in the back.

Eagin fumbled with his arms full of his son. His pants ballooned at the waist. Vomited apple made a pendent on his shoulder. His eyes were like old campfires.
The babe continued to choke in his arms.

"The angel is coming!"
The angel! Hardly were those words out when an image out of Da Vinci, its one steel eye, felt Wee Person's breath. Then the angel vanished.

"The angel has called the archangel!"

But the archangel was delayed. The amphitheater emptied. Finn rocked back and forth. Wee Person choked. The fire of air burned a hole in him. It burned a hole. Finn called for water. There was no ice. Finn called for ice. There was no water. He grasped wee person to his breast, called, rocked, prayed, wept, was angered, pathetic.

Days

P
A
S
S
E
D

Summer turned to winter and back to summer.
Spring came. Finn could hear the little bells as
Groundhogs ran out of holes. Rocks rolled by,

An avalanche revealed its beard.
It was heated by the babe's fire.
"Didadidadida," he cried.

The angel spoke to the wee lad.
"And how are you today? What's your name?"
"Didadidadida," he cried.
"How are you" said the angel.
"I'm Dr. Hopeso and this is my husband, Frog."
Frog burped in his beaker.
"Have you had a good day?"
Flannigan rocked the child.
The tongue depressor said hummm!
Steel eyes withdrew.
The amphitheater emptied.
The floors got cleaner.
Little dogs pulling buffers rounded corners.
Attendants followed in their tracks.
The room was light, cleaner than white.
It was getting to be a very clean day.
Seasons passed. The child, bare to the waist
shivered in the cool breezes of Elysium.
Finn folded him his blanket arms, hands were shirts, belly a
pillow.
 Spring came again.
Red buttons bloomed on the shelf.
The stainless steel grass was cut.
A pregnant woman x-rayed big and little Finn, his lungs, front and
side.
The season passed. The angel, the archangel returned.
Wee Person wheezed.
"We want to send him to Children's Heaven."
The ambulance meter had reached $750.
Eight white men prepared to launch.
The meter ran.
No voices were raised.

"Do you have insurance?
…Are you employed?"
Back to the amphitheater.
The fire burned.
They were just out of water
Finn thought.

They called him a cab.
It happened again.
At dinner time the babe recovered.
They gave him mixed vegetables.
 It was a cure.

Praise the LORD, you angels
Praise the LORD, all heavenly host
Praise the LORD, his works in every dominion
Praise the LORD, my soul.

Call

*Call it the big one. Call Linda Quick. Call the hard drive.
Call the Middle East. Call the invisible a parchment overwritten
with other words. Call the conquered what the conquerors are.*

The little blue jar made an alarm. Knives were in the kitchen, sticks
along the wall, a screw gun, the OED and the jar on the ledge were
on call. The neighborhood of Mother Earth rang ten at the breaking,
but it could have been more when that *sleeper lurched naked to the
bathroom door.* The light shot on.

An arm was winding in the casement window. It looked like a snake,
held the screen in its hand. Bellows filled the hood. Not the Blood, it
was him. Neighbors trooped to phones and called. The tentacle
gripped and gnawed with the screen. This orifice mauled the air.
Nothing worse was seen in war. The dogs of pity swarmed. He was
just reaching for the arm to pull its cord when it spoke:

"GO AHEAD! CALL!
CALL!
CALL THE POLICE!"

Was it a snake at all? He picked up the screen and put it in the hall.
It was the arm of a man! The battle urge rose from mere and moor,
but reason tread it down. Deductions beat their beasts. Visors fell.
Spurt the bloke and leave it on the floor?
What a mess of the would-be corpse.
Lash it to the window?
Drag it over to the ditch?
One neighbor had left a carpet there.
Behead the spout, geld it to a chair?
Or catch the nearest way?
The voice ground on, "CALL. CALL"

He dialed wrong. Try again. The angels took off their hats.
"What is your emergency?"
"A burglar's coming in my bathroom window."
"Is he in? Is he in? Stay on the line."

He slammed down the phone, but it leapt up, ringing.
"Stay on the line, stay on the line." It went dead.
This is a true story.
Then it rang again. "Please stay on the line."
"I was on the line, you hung up!"
"We were disconnected.

Are you Eagin O'Arthur Flannigan Finnigan of Pied Cow town? Is
this your number?" A computer pealed at the tone.
"Do you have Blue Cross or other insurance? Are you employed?"
Confetti blew out of the phone.

Before Finn could do more to mark the snake, bottle rockets, sky
rockets lit the lawn.
He opened the door with a frying pan.
One hatless uniform stood on the grass.
"Have you seen it, do you have a gun?"

Eyes widened. Hands tightened.
He turned on the porch light but the snake had gone.

There were pits and holes, bubble cars, plain cars, a helicopter, fire engines and a van. Seven flashlights lit O'Arthur's face.

"Did you report an emergency?
What's your name.
Do you know him?
Where does he live?"

Adrenaline shot out their ears.
An officeress offered to cuff O'Arthur to her breast for her milk.
Talk! *Fill in the card*, she said.
She threatened to leave, reneged for his social security.
Fill in the card. She offered to chop a hole in his shrubbery.
Stop a hole!
Her arms were bald as eggs. She felt the putty of his windows. The grass groaned and the bay tree splintered. Shadows beat like mothy sheep. A helicopter beat its blades. A car drove up.

"We got him!"

O'Arthur went down for the ID show.
A shirtless felon waved at the intersection.
Flashlights shined out of its ears.
It looked like a Snake O' Lantern.

O' Arthur took off his shirt.
The snake writhed its tongue, black with coffee markings, scales heaving.
The tentacles hung like arms.
The face was handsome.
The tongue flickered.
The smell was sticky.
The tail twisted.

"I just saw one arm," O'Arthur insisted. "I thought it was a snake but the fingers were popping."

Patrolmen took prints. Females gave out cards.
Men with arms like boots stamped butts in the yard.

Flashlights snapped to belts.
Patrol said, "if these prints are developed tonight they'll be ready in
six months."

The snake went on to hibernate.
O'Arthur went to hydrate, closed the window, slept awake.

Writing On the Wall

*History of rewriting as interpolation, artificial memory with
bricolage, palimpsest, hetroglossia but best carnivalization to
reorder a series of finite involuntary memories forgotten in folklore.
The Oxidant culture is a vast memory that rewrites itself as its own
freak, redo.*

ESL once lined metropolis, blasted eight feet off the ground.
Acrobatic block-long wigglers like engravings covered freeways,
signs.
Then it disappeared.
What happened?
Civilization waxing?
Democracy made safe?
City Sandblast and Paint fell vacant.
The writing was extinct.

Triumph's come, they boasted, but mind forged, engraved in walls, it
penetrated down to bone in invisibly soul-marred boys. You
could imagine the original, but the outside now was gone.
How did the writing off the wall get down into the bone?

Sure there's time before the blood-brain barrier bursts.
 ESL is syntax, not just verse, it's hieroglyphs like Mayan.
 People glad Johnny readin' sure, that's a good sign.
But we need some cats to sandblast Johnny's mind.

Johnny's a palimpsest, that's where the writing went in eye and ear
in hypertext,
it don't mean Johnny's reading when he's read to death.

Deliberate beneath the "paint," and look in Johnny's head.
That's what Saint Blake did. He said these days a net would cover
mind, called a Promethean to break the chain, the world wide web.

Don't put him down for Microsoft. He left his will engraved.

Downfall of the Demonots

*The ruin at Rogers Trough in the Superstitions is inside a
cave. It's a nice trail through trees about 4 miles from the trailhead,
easy enough to google directions. Angel Springs just a bit farther is
where Ted DeGrazia burned a million dollars of his paintings in the
70's.*

They are called Superstition Demonots from three rules of order in
the philosopher Hegel, a dialectic known as the *Golden
Superstitions*, but in reverse.

Their *third* order is at the top, called **Man Who Is**, but
hypothetically, for Demonots do not believe in such a being.

The closest explanation they give is, Is Is, Is?
　　Which is to say, Is, Is Not.
　　They believe in not being.

Since Demonots disbelieve the third order they substitute it with the
second, **Man Who Is Not**.
　　This is the man who says, Was, Is, to delve the metaphysic.

Second order initiates engage the science of nemesis.
　　It shows ironic self-awareness.

A spider caught in a web, prevented by itself from being itself, they achieve a brotherhood of the imperfect.

They are not what others think them.

They are not what they're supposed to be.

They are not what they think themselves.

In topsy turvy, **Not Man Who Is**, of the *First* Order, a Demonot underclass, took the Second and substituted itself. This Not-Man concocted *a pretend order* that said since the *Second* thought itself unworthy, it must be, for who would know better?

So the First substituted itself for the Second and pretended to be the Third.

The Secret Life of Democrats

The ordinary embedded in romantic movements presumes a sober existence in order to embrace it as good, but once again, under the ordinary eldritch presumed, civilization as a vertigo of Benjamin's quaint hieroglyphics and enigmas on top of common life, many subtle windings tell this tale and at the same time throw over it a certain coloring of the ordinary presented in an unusual way. We have no intention to reveal what the crime is. This fairy tale is still aborning, but if it slips out, too bad. Philosophies of porridge range up and down the chain of discontent. The particular house of the OOps on Willetta and the mythic ginger house of the Dame is one world for those who dwell below. Snow White tasted this porridge and fell asleep. Falling asleep means taken with the tale.

A true Democrat is a priest of the imagination.

I was sixteen when that society first battled evil in the world.

But we fell to our own nemesis, truth in opposition to the world.

Initial discussions, before corruption, were sworn to secrecy.

Those days were leaked as a version of truth, but no one pledged fidelity to betrayals, much less the twisted later events. Democracy gives that right to everyman. More openness than this is not conceived. Our openness was a cloak. Who else would be deep in the mountains at noon in full sun, among rocks under hawks to take orders? The betrayals, if I have to judge interpretations, concern later events. A final disclaimer, I knew nothing of those dread decades of existence.

I was concerned for the children of democracy when I undid a corner fence. This provoked a break in to my garage. They took all the tools worth mentioning, even the lawnmower from Sears. Since he was their leader I had police address my neighbor, who claimed someone else had dumped them in his yard, but the bicycle was in his room. When he later stood on the corner to glower I burglarized his house. This and many more rejections convinced him I was a true Democrat of the Order,
so I pretended to tutor him in the craft. Who knows best its opposition?
I gathered these secrets before he went to prison.

Democrasy

As with hieroglyphics of ancient Mayan, writing that radiates about a center, as Whorf has also said of Hopi, the writing on walls fades with time, creating, a writing over writing, a palimpsest effect called *democrasy*. Democrasy undergirds that inner fourth level. Sometimes scholarship, but often innuendo and gossip is well hidden beneath the mask. Authorities do not credit the outer order as viable, and acknowledge nothing of the inner. To the untutored eye democrasy is as indecipherable as writing on the wall, for *the sentence that begins in the east may only be completed in the west*

Originally Democrats were assassins, then became burglars, which philosophical impoverishment is attributed to the youth market. Apprentice burglars attempt to qualify for the inner order which Levy-Bruhl concedes is invisible but uses apprentice labor. The ages of apprentices correspond to our junior high school, which should not imply lack of sophistication. Single-parent homes supply cars and trunk space in house and yard for the booty, called "chumpo" in democrasy. Homes loosely governed by older siblings initiate themselves in pure alibi, space and transport. *Ah gainy ma, Chum, po!* it is said. Neighborhood apprentices operate as pack vendors. Their victims are older women mostly, infirm deer pulled down by majority ethos.

Prey

A widow stranded in the veldt, whose home retains amenities from her husband's efforts at the good life, fruit trees, hedges, gardens, fences, which first gave her security, are weakened by children begging to pick the figs, oranges, apricots and grapefruits, ply the lady with piteous looks and pleas for pomegranate to report the presence and location of marketable items. Continuous erosion of fences produces entry at four or five places. The apprentice scout confirms the spoor and plots the lady's movement, when she goes for a walk or visits her daughter. New safety glass regulations ensure no sound of breaking glass or that a Democrat will be injured.

Entry by the window, exit by the door. First break-ins take the toasters, portable TVs, jewelry, money. Second, third and fourth breakings, for Democrats are trained in serial burglary, take stereos, VCRs, washers and dryers. It is curiously not so long from planting a peach tree to the loss of your refrigerator.

This Darwinism of initiates is contradicted if a less vulnerable person moves to the address. Then the apprentices, failing to adapt quickly, may fall prey themselves. An increasing yuppie population need not trouble the Democrat who considers this golden age, but the arrest of Democrat burglars is foreseen and desired by the inner order as a test. If an apprentice is given a police record that ensures he will become an adjunct member, an affiliate for odd chores, though not inner circle material. If the apprentice goes uncaught until 18, he is sent to college and law school.

When promising apprentices appear an inner circle woman rents a home in the hood outfitted with video and sound to record their performance. She makes herself vulnerable and when the strike occurs it is analyzed for merit by the promotion committee. This also benefits the goods claimed for insurance, even if that stored as bait is damaged and does not work. Thus business and government, legislatures and churches teach discrimination.

Democracy among the implicit hashishim of the 12th century, the Templar Knights, and Egyptian tombs suggest to Graves its roots back to Anubian jackals. Moderns see it coincident with New Deal legislation. Democrat media uses time tested anthropologists like Louden Perry to say, "the fig tree founded the industrial revolution."

Democrat society is anti-discrimination. This covers the greater paradox. The victim is taken as the thief and the thief treated like the victim. The old lady says she lost a sewing machine, her nephew's bicycle, a skill saw and a lawn chair, but they are only returned after a minutely perfect description and receipts. Possession is nine tenths of the law.

By their wealth inner circle theorists and legislators attract outsiders to **a tripling of Democrat influence**. The only empirical clue in scientific literature that even points to the inner order's existence was in the work of Jimson, whose tendency toward violet and purple, even pink in the choice of foreign special issue automobiles implied a compensatory sensuality commensurate with familial deprivation.

It is not wise to trifle with the innocent youth spotting furniture in your neighborhood. They may become a general, a senator, an executive. A ribald paradox of Tit Corp, maker of subliminal telecom appliances, revealed that all its board members were initiates, but who found that they made less profit because of it! All professions are represented except insurance.

Probationary Inner Circle

Duplicity is easily taught to quick young minds. THERE ARE MANY CIRCLES IN THE SUPERSTITION SPIRAL. Perhaps the two single most important are the rituals of face changing and the invisibility cloak.

Face Changing

Face changing comes more or less naturally. Democrats are taught to CHANGE THE THOUGHT AND THE FACE WILL FOLLOW. Probationers undergo exercises to produce this result. Paired off they are told to convince their partner that black is white, or white is black, which means that they must fervently believe it themselves. These are no smiling villains, but those who believe with all their Loyola hearts and souls that their thought is the epitome of sincerity. Lady Macbeth might look like the innocent flower but be the serpent under it, but the probationer is THE GOOD IN EVIL repeated so many times to convince that any exigent course is right.

All probate Democrats can pass lie detector tests. Those who believe in the classical training of the curriculum review the heroic moments of Achilles' madness and Ulysses' guile, foreshortened in the renaissance masters of the Borgias, Hamlet and Faustus, including the sublime moments in early espionage from Bruno and Marlowe to Trithemian codes. This is all conducted with that modern heuristic device, the Hav-ard Case Method.

Invisibility

The invisibility cloak is not so easily learned. It too is a form of shape change but involves the whole body. A probationer is expected to stand downtown at midday outside his place of business and not be seen as his coworkers go to lunch. The skill is not commonplace.

The emphasis is upon thinking reality into that shape we desire it to take. A Democrat learns to PROJECT SIMULTANEOUS CONTRADICTION, which process is often labeled the three Ms,

Misdirecting the observer's attention,
Mirroring the observer's attention,
Manipulating the observer's attention.

The 3 Ms are immensely aided with a theta brain rhythm. Since perceived reality is a misimpression created by the observer, it is not so difficult to confuse it further.

Misdirecting the observer's attention is easily done as a trick of simple household magic. You can do it yourself the next time somebody asks you a tough question. **Merely ask for the question to be repeated.** Note the different and easier language the second time, mostly because your respondent is trying to help you since you are both tedious and simpleminded. Also, many a thievery has occurred with the acquiescence of the owner merely by the thief's asking, **"you don't want this do you?"** The simple audacity covers the theft which is out the door before the answer occurs.

Mirroring the observer's attention means that since people see what they want to see and nobody would rather see anything but themselves, help them to **see** what they want by acting it out, mere **do** the opposite. Seeing vs. doing.

Manipulating is the most difficult to practice because it requires misdirecting and mirroring first. The idea is to **turn the point** to your advantage. Consider that a new sewer system will save the environment and it will also *change the zoning.*

Zoning

All these techniques together are called Zoning, but to the rank and file probationer the difficulty comes in believing that the process of **Zoning works when we don't see it work**. Obviously however if it is seen to work the practitioner has been caught.

Invisibility is only completed by the mysterious fifth level Master. An instance occurred in the vast hierarchy of Superstition Democrats when the probationers went to perform the ritual tea ceremony in the state rotunda at midnight. The master is reported to have seen the guard quizzically examine his left shoe top when he passed the scene.

Naturalistically we would expect some such thing anyway since THE MORE BIZARRE AN EVENT the more it is denied. What

Democrats have achieved collectively in this in sixty years instructs us in the profundity and profitability of even the superficial bizarre in instances of invisibility. INVISIBILITY LEADS TO INVINCIBILITY say the teachers, citing the mythological example of that Cabal of the D.C. Capitol.

First Circle Governance Initiates

Fourth level initiates have succeeded in the techniques above. This is the highest level that can be perceived by the unformed Democrat who tends to idolize, even worship these high beings. They, like gods brought to the pinnacle of **perfected duplicity and counterfeit, exclusively compromise the ruling and monied class,** hence their attractiveness.

All first circle governance initiates today are upper level professionals, administrators, executives and managers. Here they can do the most good for themselves and for the order in manipulation, control, modifying and enriching those they are serving. Many undertake philanthropy. Nonprofit NGOs in the arts, education and science receive major funding from the order which is furthered while all opposition is automatically considered to be a liar by media plants and the law. This is not so much by conspiracy as the psychology that **whoever opposes the truth must be a liar!**

Invisible Democratic Masters

While the fifth level masters are invisible and unknown, in a way we may say more of them than any other level. Unfortunately it is impossible to discover whether any of it is true. There is an abundance of myth, new and old, but what empirical data? We may find Hesiod's belief in the eternal old men of the golden age to be analogous. These likewise invisible persons would intervene and preserve justice when necessary. Surrealists of course take the more skeptical view that the absence of a thing does not imply its inference.

Democrat deconstructuralists believe that the opposite of a thing is the most probable cause, meaning the **opposite of expectation**. They argue that if human fantasy expects the numinal, then the reality is the practical, the domestic, the everyday. These say, like the Reactive Alchemists, that the baser matter is gold, but take the opposite of what is believed. This school has gained the greatest following in recent years among the inner orders where the first principle is to seek the world in opposition to the truth. Here the assumption is that the world is a matrix of diametrically opposed opposites.

Demo Box

From this philosophy came the invention of the now much acclaimed Demo Box, a series of paradoxes where the successful solution—not to have begun to play—resides in neither gold nor lead, and not in-between, but **nowhere**. The point was made by Jimson as well, but we know what happened to him! Saying that the truth is nowhere is tantamount to saying it is invisible, meaning it is impossible to apprehend by ordinary senses. What we are left with is fantasy, authority and theory. These have their minute popularities before they fade into the Babylonian (Budge).

The implicit nihilism of the Box should not trouble us nearly as much as its mythological bias. Demo Box is diagrammed as a decline from a focus, a series of slanted lines with an inverted center like a lava crater. You can also see the likeness in Plato's cave. Why beings with egress from this paradox remain within is not clearly defined. They will neither leave or disbelieve.

One absurd view argues that since we believe in them the masters do not exist, but that if they do we do not see them because they masquerade among us in impossible disguises as uninitiates.

Recent fiction has taken the view that the master is a Quixote, riding through the desert singing ridiculous odes upon his horse's back, trampling wildflowers, polluting clear waters with unclear and managing to betray those very principles held dear by Democrats everywhere, to mock and to rock this extremity.

The master is pictured as a German tourist at the Grand Canyon parked in a Cruise America Winnebago that chugs its auxiliary motor stupidly in the night while he barbecues chicken. Indeed to go as far as possible, if the master is the most repugnant species, a Wisconsin snowbird. These fictions show the extreme need for Democrats to conceptualize the nobodies who govern them.

Zoning and the Superstition Spiral

A positive result of this philosophizing was the definition of the Superstition Spiral. For the Democrat all matter must relate from the dead zone, what we should consider as the point of least elevation from which the spiral comes. The Dead Zone is opaque to sunlight and light, though its citizens manage to make it seem otherwise by placing ingenious plastic shrubbery.

Opaque sun and rain means that in the Dead Zone the sun does touch the earth but is reflected from a Domed atmosphere. Rain, called impervious runoff, is channeled into large tanks where it is stored for basic needs and manufacturing.

The Dead Zone Zoning proceeds outward and downward we should say. Democrats consider its movement lateral, as zone mystics do inward, as much as up and down. As the spiral expands it encompasses territory like the Dantean system until the First Circle is complete.

Fourth level initiates live in the first circle where they can best oversee the DISINTEGRATION OF THE ORIGINAL ORDER of things. This entropy is the whole purpose of Democratic society in its Manifest.

Initiates believe like the anthropologists that they are the "transient efflorescence of a creation in relation to which they have no meaning' (Levi-Strauss), except of course in profit taking, hence the overpowering need to disintegrate structures so that they are no longer capable of integration.

The number of circles in the Superstition Spiral is not fixed because there is free travel between them and because the incessant subdivision of territory makes for new, if after all, homogenous categories.

Understand however that ALL MATTER IS CONSIDERED SUBJECT TO DEMOCRACY.

Hence our German national grand master is simultaneously a resident of Zone 3, North Europe, and of the high country of Zone 3. Zoning theory more or less resembles a system of correspondences that suit a medieval feudal governance. Numbers, plants, planets, stars, modes of behavior, dress, activities, arts and all natural and unnatural substance correlate to their origin in the Dead Zone but also take separate identity in the extended system. For example the number zero, cholla, Mars, Andromeda, insipidity, shirtlessness, campers and cowboy are endemic but also extend in modified form to other zones.

Multiple metamorphoses characterize both the spiral and the Dead Zone and are a complete study in themselves.

Conclusions

The nameless fears of citizen groups against land developers, zoning commissions, political parties, boards of every kind, governors, mining companies and conglomerates at every level are more justified than any of them suspects in his worst nightmare.

The Democrat System so interpenetrates the social fabric that the worst possible case is not at all accurate, for who suspects churches of complicity or charities or universities? These however by a logical extension must be the repositories of the highest most deceitful initiates of the fourth level.

The social body being so shot through with degeneration, a certain stoic acceptance behooves the investigator. After all, what is the point of complaining to Democrats about Democrats?

But a worse is yet to come, for you see, applying the law of opposites, that what is true is the opposite of what is intended, we must find that this treatise itself is a production of that Society which augers a golden age for all.

Further we must say that those who praise the good are ill and that those who are ill are ill. The highest a Democrat can reach is the opposite of good intent. Nemesis is certain in the Demo Box where THE ONLY SOLUTION IS NOT TO PLAY.

For only those who are silent are knowing, only those who are invisible are real and only those who are foolish are wise.

The Lime Rat Probe

Kafka says in Amerika that Karl Rossman "gave a few side kicks to flatten a rat...but merely succeeded in driving it more quickly into its hole, for though he had very long legs they nonetheless weighed him down." (Harman, 10). This might advise state use of spy cameras, geo phones, illumined grid life surveillance cameras and microphones intercepts that the Ubu Attorney General used in prosecutions and later for writing his memoirs. Kafka's diary entry in 1911 says, "I was so incoherent this morning, I felt nothing but my forehead...would simply have curled up on the cement floor of the corridor...but my body is too long for its weakness" (Tremendous World, 30). *Grandfathers in Esquilache. Madrid, 1766, smashed 4400 oil burning streetlamps twelve feet high in protest against illumination.*

First. Thousands of these prod cells are undetected at the macro mart.To call them cells is inaccurate in the plural.
Just one prod makes a cell. They are at the borders.

Second. In the world of six, prod cells contingency plan with the mind of prods
but are not a mind. When those cell(s) form the odd number, three young, they immerse themselves in the language, geography, skills, and goals of prods and plan as prods plan, or not, for prods may not plan as they ought, or as their leaders would.

Three. Expect the ensuing prod act to take documents and official tactics to infiltrate non-scenes.
Here the definition of non-scene is difficult.

Four. Because three means six it is impossible to identify cell numbers. I fell asleep at midday once and woke to see Prods in a van at an army school. This was beyond belief. Hopefully the prods fell asleep again.

Five. You would think you could call out to the In in them, that is, to the prods diffuse, divert:
"Come now you prods," you would assert, but….

Six. We are being innerwhelmed.

Note: They got their name from their port of entry, Point Produgal. Or Prodicul, or Protigull. Analysis shows either and all explains it.

Prod Probe *Foonnote*

The Lime Rat Probe has nought to do with pigs. You get tired of explaining it. A captured prod would shed some light. Who can't make that claim? The Swine. Di prado ate the pig. Did prodos eat the pig? Huh? Hardly! Among different kinds there exist a droop, a jack, and a prod. Prod's ruse all right. This message was found on their doors.

Training Hege for the Maze

Approaching the maître d, a man is asked, sir have you reservations? Yes, he replies, "Hegel for two." Hegelian dialectic is an urban legend of two extremes to force a choice between. Old abandoned beds of rivers forced to change, keep in your walls. The Seine, Euphrates hardly break from substrate when, thesis here, counter thesis there, a reviver, then a bend, not the Colorado rusing to salt sea, elaborate idyll ambiguity, but Hegel to text. Who belongs to the Thames? This window I soon shut and into my chamber am gone.

Hegel, **as you know**, was head coach of the Chargers. He had to consider offense and defense equally, which dualism resolved in his entertainment of the hypothetical third, that being his audience where forces blended.

Thesis, antithesis synthesis, strophe, antistrophe, stand. Even the Mighty Blake said *without contraries there is no progression,* revealing the fairy backgrounds of his amorphous seed. That's why Joyce said

> Transmogrify, transmogrify,
> if not the eagle will come and pull out your eye.

Joyce said that and coaches and government scientists were getting it. Morpheus, Amorphous, fire and water sloshed, male and female divided the *Symposium*. But androgyne lips shut by light and dark, death and life. Ludwig Wittgenstein the Great, whose head rests on a pedestal in the Denver air park, said, "can that which is not be, not be, simultaneously?" Thus the law of noncontradiction was the *bête noire* of scientists who could not overcome the irrelevance in programs, like those that edited out "Junk" DNA.

It shows imagination to call DNA junk. Swish! Some 50 % of the noncoded DNA genome, wasn't black or white. Non-binary QED broke Hegel's boundaries, which continued until the Russians clicked in DNA consciousness, Bearden's Zarg if you must know, **that 90% of the so-called junk DNA was a language itself!** Post-quantum mechanics (PQM), BOOM!

I don't know how many of you store the *Principia* (PM) in your garage near the car in case the incompleteness theorem comes.

Illumination of the Maze

The key word in all this maze is '**modeling**' neuro-linguistic programming term (NLP), in the technology of intelligence control, or simply a syndrome called the Werther effect

where if Werther kills himself if you do.

"In NLP texts, a hypnosis is elaborated where two therapists – one speaking mostly at random in one ear, while the other gives specific instructions into the other – **confuse a subject's conscious mind into 'shutting down,'** thus bringing the unconscious mind to the fore in a state of trance."

Then what! With Werther the observed behavior of any figure may be adopted. **Model** anything, but be the serpent under it.

Efforts are being made to change the name of NLP to DHE™ = Design Human Engineering™] (Baber, I), "simultaneous installation strategies [that] defy old beliefs about building NEW feelings... ones not experienced, yet" (La Valle). These broken boundaries rupture the intestine wall, a being with bags of itself sticking out has a certain **automaticity** to it.

No matter what, the leftovers from paradoxical sets of Russell's Antimony where **a thing is not a member of itself** discovered this contradiction.

The modern absolutism of science gave urban Hegelians more power to build maze thought, called the Amazery, **a Dome** that banishes paradox as a means of hiding it, held as we do the **camouflage theory** of the human principle, *what is there hid shall be shouted.*

True believers are wanted. Borges flatboats and round boats will go down Philosophy River like Mississippi barges hauling large statutes of Borges to be set up in each new crevice.

Doesn't it help to know that from the air the maze looks like a flower? Remember, on completion of his mission, the Manchurian candidate committed suicide. Current crops may just blank out.

These are all parables of the **paradox of self-reference** which obviate the self and its consciousness for some other.

It must be an Aristotelian metaphysic that Dante cites about the Donation of Constantine where the Emperor is not free to do through an office assigned him anything contrary to the office since it would be contrary to itself.

The Law of Identity says identity must be consistent with itself. A trick question is, who shaves the barber in this maze? Which in our terms might be the same as asking whether the Trans human class is or is not a member of itself. Can the human which is, not be?

In ours the barber grows a beard. If a "list of all lists that do not contain themselves" contains itself, then it does not belong to itself and should be removed. However, if it does not list itself, then it should be added to itself."

That is exactly the position of Hegelian synthesis and Schrödinger's cat, inventions of nihilists who keep the maze.

Whether the cat is simultaneously dead or alive Coleridge said death in life cocktails were drunk by Amazants to practice quantum entanglement, as though Schrödinger and Einstein exchanged heads with their letters.

Head-letters of quantum superposition are **the system definitely in one state we can consider as being partly in each of two or more other states**.

This describes the maze as perfectly as it does **macro societal alters** and personal ones. As long as you consider these you consider those. Ur, keep thinking.

Schrödinger has also a mouse in that lab and a bear in the cage outside, with stacks of chimps unopened. These are the philosophers, gurus and grants who coach illumination.

TRUMPBALALABAMM! Seeing the Angel Poet

  --In some texts Balaam is sued for striking the ass. More up to date on the prescient, there he is in front of his ass, arms raised in a

v. The pillar of light beside him is the angel. That we have difficulty seeing these figures is the point, for Balaam cannot see the angel but the ass can. Context with the paranormal Balaam the motto of poets, who like angels, once they get their ass to braying, develop ass thought and circumstance to TrumpBalalabamm's playing.

Laban's angel is the next best laugh until we get to Balaam. Our Father Maimonides saw the spirit and seraphim in the most wicked of men. Laban, *the most perfectly wicked man,* violated all the righteous, but Balaam tops him. *Guide of the Perplexed* says an ass had to see the spirit first. Laban. Balaam. Ass. Who's next?

Ding an sich, my friends, explains the molecules and name. Nothing is really there when the ass goes to consult its betters. This is an ass of the upper crust, no mere donkey. Maimonides calls it Seer. On this prophet Balaam sat; it was his eyeglass to see the angel. You think it a joke, man-straddle? This our fathers do not say.

Here the indignity is a whirling sword in the path. Balaam *chose the better part* and beat the ass with a stick. He beat the stick, he beat the ass, he beat himself. Things come in threes. Swords flashed. The ass turned into a wall. I don't mean it became a wall but in turning to avoid the angel it ran into a wall. Balaam kicked it with his foot.

The ass saw the sword a third time when Balaam had yet to see it once. The ass went down on a knee. That's history. Balaam beat it with a book. On long roads there's a lot to read. But while the perfect ass was dumb, it was not blind, and conversely Balaam could talk. He filled the air with oaths. He was a poet. His blind eye flew open when the ass began to plead, which sounded just like Buñuel pounding out the song he knew so well, "I thank God I am an atheist, ho, ho, ho." This of course became, "I am, thank God, an atheist *nevermore.*" Obsessed with the Bible, overcome by sight, he saw every word unspeakable carved on the naked eye. Buñuel, Laban, Balaam, Ass, fill in your name.

To interpret, Balaam's sin is the military industry, which is why the angel said, *I come here to oppose.* Strike up the band. This proverb of the paranormal Balaam, who cursed God and got blessed, is the perfect motto for poets who, as angels, will have their way. Men do get an ass to speaking, but when will it stop? As to the task of ass thought, its circumstance and braying, we do not doubt it is an ass poem playing. That's *nothing new under sun.* Along side we hear Balaam's trombone.

Notes:

*–Laban most wicked of men.-*Maimonides, Guide of the Perplexed, II, 195f

–No atheist any more. -Buñuel and Dali in *Un Chien Andalou* (1929) cut the eye with a razor. Dali accused Buñuel of being an atheist and a communist over the unconsciousness carcass on the piano in that film. Buñuel could have been murdered like Lorca had he stayed in Spain, but he deconfessed his atheism, "it's guilt we must escape from, not God." *El ángel exterminador* (1962) Exterminating Angel (1962), is a symbolic holocaust.

-I come here to oppose. Numbers 22.32.

–Balaam. Numbers 22-24.

Saurian Limo

If I said I saw a rhinoceros run across the piano it would make as much sense as this Limo, but might be taken as a joke we have been thinking of and just now blurted out to ask what the status of thought is vs. actually seen. Well it was actually seen, apropos of nothing, so that days later it was modeled and fired and glazed and fired and now it is out of the kiln and sits on the table being too big for the piano even in this reduced state we can ask does it look like the rhino on the piano which only existed for a second? Of course this is real, but it was real enough to become real so it was real then too? This havoc to the game of recognition, and sequence and reasonable information vs nonsense, to doubt the reasonable or the reason, indeed is open to doubt whether counterfeits in a labyrinth of

robots of cell tower trees, that look like trees, and cell tower church
bell towers are real. Then what in the world is the rhino on the piano
but a joke we haven't told yet, are telling now in the Limo.

As my earplugs got looser I began to hear gossip from the noisy
world. Rumors were that when the Saurians came to resettle the old
world, which was economical even if darkness had begun, a new
cycle came. Energy was left you see and the crocs took endless
flights to repopulate the dust worlds after the crickets had gone.

Croc authors divide the visible air into snap and bite. All were
snapping so cacophony dismayed our duck migrants and pigeons.
When they landed on bent wires the poles melted to the ground.
Pods snapped and each dust clap made three or four clamoring lights
to rise in a single wet, then fall. Where would it end? The motes of
dust led the insects a hundred to one. Everything was dust. In the
dust settling from another blow the lizards chomped in the yard
where crickets were all pealing, "no, no eat me!" What moved those
stateless grasshoppers the bobwar fence? Creeping where ants dare
go, reaching collars, under sills, into light sockets: "ants are biting
me."

Ants tunneled under the hill and Aussies sand-blasted their mutton.
Dust rained in hand claps. Sand piles were filling.
Steel rods struck the rivers of blood, when there was water to bleed.
Nutrient blood flowed down all dust and mixed with flesh,
nutritious and pleasing to crops, barley feed down the Salt.
The Department of Corrections has proved that this true on all
planets, but not on small stars. Some thought these were blood, but
others thought them diamonds of wide need.

Pied Cow was rich in Phosphate. Dumps of soot and stone had built
up stuff into a pile of trucked earth.
Make the bump!
Away with the flat!

Into this wide need seas flowed.

Round rain balls and duct tears, globes to live and die would lose another world.

Pity the poor crickets and stone lizards their teachers. The lizard child winked its eye at me. It had a student cricket between its jaws as if to say,

> I know the passing of the dust,
> the great bumps of rock
> and the mountains yet to come.
> Say boy, could you start up that hose!

He leapt up to shoulder height then and did a little dance, wearing short pants and a hat with a diagram of stars. But then a saurian limousine, two crocodiles mating, swept up in a rush and swallowed the little friend. Oh the digestible horrors of it when he passed through worlds of gastric and came out in a swamp.

In this consciousness of toes, where the dust rivers come to sit in peace, one said:
"I was an amillennial Lutheran enzyme, a fence row two feet down, anaerobic for centuries. This rising swept me up truck tops. My beauty gems the grasses, who is like me?"

Do not overlook this populace of the nebular level where wee people wander, fingers popping, hands snapping, "snapper come!" You will find out yourself. Up and away the Boombay kings carried it to the sun and buried air in the ear. The grasshoppers were celebrating with umbrellas and the wee people danced under the croton.

Misadventures of Tom Goat's Shout in Space

I was voted co-chairman of the AGSE preemptive house union of 600 TAs who taught all the undergrad English classes at UT-Austin. My program was to promote poetry readings and pay the recipients. Tom Goar appeared in the one where the distinguished John Lehmann, secretary of Virginia Woolf and Edith Sitwell, read. The copy Goat had in his bound Poems, 1969-72 is the one referred to below, but "Prospero, Sweet Prince," was also arranged to appear in **Lucille 3**, *edited by Gunner Chainsaw Hansen. All this to remind us that Ophelia, Polonius, Prospero, highwire, Hamlet and "Ahad stalking the deck in the wind," make poetry something else. The SHOUT is not even in Lucille, or in the Poems, but it was in that room, suddenly, a shout at the top of his voice. It scared them all. As a token and I'm thinking to reissue them all in case we need to heap uf apocalypse.*

After 50 years of eye smoke, you resemble something much like this fellow here.
Francelia becomes a storm....she screams to life...she opens her eye to the fury of dawn.

He comes shouting. He was still alive then. Turn the page. Some *lady knitting red long johns* leaps over from the *New York Times*. She is Blues From Room 7 with *silver zephyrs sweeping stars*, and angels.

Now the angels look down from their rooftops to see. What do they see, Naropa?

Laugh in the dark, you Hungry Mother Monument.

Somebody call Bly, tell him Pegasus is loosed from the neck Medusa Perseus slew!

Sea foam down in the deep heart's core, *below in the center / the molten mother's lava heart-core flows.* Skip the geologic. What a relief.

It doesn't say the Lord descended.
It doesn't say the flowers bloomed.
It doesn't say wars will cease.
The war's on it says.

So he says, *I took it down, / Put it in my blood, everything you said.* Like when they're out of ink and can't write no more 'less they tap a vein, or out of water can't drink, no blankets to wrap a shrink, shivering with no meds, we get carrots out of a bag for our old dog, broccoli stems and lettuce, New York strip, fry eggs with bacon and lunch meat. It's cheaper than MRIs.

How many MRIs have you had? *I became Ahab stalking the deck in the wind...and it made me so cold.* That's when I thought he would bring up Ophelia again, Ophelia who drowned, I said to myself, Ophelia who got married when she was old... *Ophelia, I have lived too long-- / Now I am Polonius / Remembering the arras.*

Memory memory on the wall who the freakest of them all?

That's a question, but the answer is *when daylight started cracking through my walls I was a fool!*

Dear Harriet, Wallace said,

"I see no objection to cutting down...your criticism is clearly well-founded (183)...I should prefer to keep the lines unchanged..." (Wallace Stevens, *Letters*, 184).

But then *I felt a chill / A shattering blast of a trumpet whose time has come*, but no sound echoes the year, blasts ground, circles up, goes down. The scream, the shout, the blast to keep from echoing I adjust the TV at night to Off! Flip the switch, the main switch, cut the cable, call the soul's end from sounds I cannot hear, set out to calculate the velocity of shout.

Figuring the rate of escape, its transit is x times the number of days out the solar heard on Betelgeuse. TV escapes earth and not The Shout? Broadcast light, sound goes out. **It translates the sublunar, heard in space before all.**

That's what beings of the Betterguese do, turn on earth at night, watch the tube. Count this multiplied by the indefinitude of shouts and it's no wonder we wear plugs to keep them out. They wear ear phones to keep them in, shouts multiplied with groans. You say how could they, how bizarre? I don't know.

But you're a living actor on the stage to read the lines apportioned you and be happy in unknowing. Happy unknowing we, there are so many words for it as Eskimos have for snow. You think it silent when you type but it is not. Audient layers orchestrate. What seascape won't reecho?

Wind wraps cold around...a voice to sing? I need a bark, to float.

His cry is octaves up, *slit my throat with shadows*, he says, so the cry too is light, *an empty chair, past understanding...Whisps of angels...let the fire freeze.*

Phrases come like waves not tsunami. Light, angels, *squeeze water from the rock*. He says, *Be rain.*

All chords, melodies scat the head voice, chest voice, toes sing with hands *from the windowpane*, a dance, not seen. Unseen, but heard, the many ways of groan. Answer to this has lived among the elk for years, as we know from travels in their realm, uncredited more than coyote songs, being hymns to the lost.

There are the lost and there are those who sing, who pad moss and turf, eye shine. Everything depends upon predation inside halls and rooms. Some night over to Green Gardens the prisoners in white gowns curl fingers, claw and gnarl the air. Voices hear, but not with the same SHOUT! this *clown whose eyes are wax...head as large, circled* in a *waving brain*. Oh wave the life of the waving world into the heart again! *The walls are membranes*, walls, ceilings, windows, doors. The floors are lost.

Memories past with the debris of lives, remain. We dig in peril through the top pain down. What about this and what about they take on and off the kimberlites? Diamonds in the crust seek memories of one regression an old man makes, one who had the bypass and the kidney out, down to where nobody knows. He lay in his life and heard the radar replaced by laser points. He makes a myth, takes off hat, hair, eyes, skin, teeth, sails to a wind of flame. Down further in the crust, over river, through woods, trees glisten. He comes out in boyhood where grass sings:

What we know is our creation. I would be still.. fade out my head. Into *the river of lights on the road* he says, *I hunger and I dream against it... become invisible as sun breaks.*

Dissolution earned, maybe merited, sought, felt, wept, to work hard for open sky, cold air, snow. Be snow, lay your hand!

The fire is opalescent first, then incandescent, with tinges of wit on the border of the kiln, so hot you shield your face. Singed eyebrows handle light in *the deeper silence of the lower brain.* And if that's the lower, above you walk in a kiln meet yourself. Nebuchadnezzar's boys roast next to the four who won't burn. I can't look, he says, *the vision dims.*

That's good for him, but it wakes me and I look at seed coats sprung off the sides of form sprayed with water as the shell flakes cool. The egg is born in its shell but doesn't last. The lake is an egg, the fawn is an egg, the leg, foot, hand reach out of the kiln to retrieve, not from fire, to retrieve from the impure remembering. Can you remember tomorrow what you were a white tail fleeing over fences? He comes out into it,

Bronze in the sun; The lion's in my tread as I walk And my mane flows behind.

These forms, three legged giraffes, spotted, tall as peaks covered with the last freeze before spring, he calls here the *time for killing.* The advantage in posthumous **knowing** is you get to test words with life, see what escapes they make two merge into sunlike weather in the arms of a wife with children around them in age. It's either this or something else.

Track down the posthumous unknown, not that you should, and ask, not that he would tell, whether to bring up the past or not. Nobody else remembers, not even him, but the last page,

Songbird singing in a shower of rain Cat sits on the porch listening, echoes and reechoes with your own in the rain that falls on rock to make a three petaled lily, an escarpment more aquifer and songbird billowed flocks of storm, hundreds, thousands of song breasts ruffed, pressed out. And the cat lies head down to follow seasons, the cat, bird, moment where pebbles clash against sand for traction, where the earth remains blue white bloom.

The word *shout* isn't capped in the text. It scared everybody to death. Thirty or 40 torn ears and bleeding toes. I heard it in that room scream shouted, universal world shouted for all the displaced *maquiladores* at their desks. Harriet Monroe said she would never to come to these things again. She wrote to Wallace, "change the text and leave out stanza 7." He acquiesced.

 Nobody said anything to Tom. The shout built momentum. It deafened him over and over. I heard it again over time. It woke me to pick up the fragments I have a copy of.

"I can blue such blues they're Down a hole to China never seen
I can blue such blues they're red Down a hole to China like I said."

Help in The Steps

This story got into to <u>FictionDaily</u> November 7, 2011 as well as Orion Headless, "If you call that any kind of life studying shadows on the wall among smoke, it reminded him of the lake at the bottom of world where he used to ...Which however posted the link in error. <u>Here is the right one </u>. (now defunct). He believed in Beowulf when scholars did not, scholars and dragons. Up and down, up and down the mere churned. If you doubt everything you have no story at all. As to being able to recognize the error of his ways, his inability

to control himself, did he have to grow back his arm?"
https://web.archive.org/web/20110619020449/http:/orionheadless.c
om:80/special-anniversary-section/ Scroll down at Wayback here

If you call that any kind of life studying shadows on the wall among
smoke, it reminded us of the lake at the bottom of world where they
used to live. He realized he was a monster, it said so right in the text,
which made him wish for the rest, but the head was gone. Who
knows, did he have the head or the body? This did not help in *The
Steps*.

*Come to believe that a Power greater than ourselves can restore us
to sanity.*

 I have the advantage on this one, he thought. He believed in a power
greater than himself, the glory hound, the heaven hound. He believed
in Beowulf when even scholars did not, scholars and dragons. Up
and down, up and down, the mere was churning with polar bears and
eels. If you doubt everything you have no story at all. As to being
able to recognize the error of his ways, his inability to control
himself, did he have to grow back his arm?

It's a little delirious to have a *searching moral inventory of yourself.*

The beastie had written in the margin, "they see life without
observing it. They see it but they don't see. They think I don't see,
but I do."

This denial caused consciousness and being to increase. The word
"buried" wasn't just scrawled, it completely obliterated the page.
That was *Step Ten*, inventory of the serious monster alive. He
sounded like the Apostle praying for delivery.

He admitted to God and himself, but where was he to find *another
human being to tell the exact nature of his wrongs?* Where was he to
find *"another human being?"* Not likely! What was he anyway but
the other without the an?

Humbly he asked to remove his shortcomings. These were not small. Now he was outside, a bird flew up in the margin. He saw a dark figure, aegis of his cry for help. The margin of the book had a series of connections missing. A bone stuck up out of a plate. OK, another shortcoming.

He added it to the list of all persons he had harmed.

Further evidence of a monster in the bush, a bird seemed to be waving a weed whacker.

Amends to injure he stood in the door.

It was like an entrance to the letter H, one line he bet Dante wished he never wrote. It said, "I'm going into the letter H," but without the bar. Monsters were all about, but the illustrated version was worse, saved only by his failure to visualize and their ability to forget. In the new age it would have been a hit he saw, as he read the hard parts, the tortures.

"If their classics are like this how do any of them pass the twelve steps?"

If you're thinking that you'd rather not go into the letter H or even the M to face this we sympathize, but can offer no assistance. H and M are two letters of the four that vexed his *continued personal inventory!* Also they were backwards, the M came before the H, which was like asking some stranger at a light whether he had ever looked into an O, but that was not one of the letters either.

If he could solve these things it would be better. The puzzle surrounded him, grappled him. Smoke, tallow, lapped at the water's edge. The mystery was not confined to the alphabet, even if the letters were almost the same, in case you don't know.

To improve his conscious contact with God as he understood Him he took the cipher of "OKU" that occurred in the right hand corner of his book as a sign. The tail of the O went through the K and paralleled the U. To him it made a "hum."

"What am I to do," he thought?
He began to hum aloud.

This correlated with the statement that "it was not unusual to hear them contradict themselves," the point of his inquiry, which was to find the end of contradiction in its beginning. It reminded him that the best proof yet that he was human was to find another being to admit it to. It reminds us all. Why can't we just say that and be done?

Having a spiritual awakening as the result of these steps he was ready to carry out the next level. He thought the Helmings deserved such action. How best to communicate? In one age the priest would become an Everyman commentator and say whatever was real or covered up.

Ur-Mon, reporter, lawyer, editor, was somebody telling you what to do. Mainly to doubt, he thought he understood. The emendation looked like the beak of a stork going after a fish. It could have been a goat with horns. Then he was looking down at Unferth as if from a crag, who didn't notice; he was busy corralling Hrothgar's sister. This hardly seemed anybody's business except it was magnificent, an into the body experience that enthralled. The sister was being offered to the man who looked anonymous in a business suit. He lay down on a bed and a carrot flew up from his legs.

The smoke made him dizzy, the smoke and feel of the fell, as if symbol and story and present and past were changed. He didn't know there were handbooks printed to get over these tough spots, to correctly see symbol and fact. You need to get the handbooks. He didn't know whether they were going to make the book into a movie.

At least, *he tried to carry this message to others, to practice these principles in his affairs.*

There was a large cursive E which also looked like a 3. It was bisecting an ampersand. This was in the book. Science called it the E3 bisect. He was new to reading. In his eyes it was a Z. He thought it looked like a dragon at the throat of another dragon, that one dragon was twisting the neck of the other out and down. He knew that was how dragons got their wings, by killing another. He could not escape carnage. To add to this plight, the girl Wealtheow, who had appeared earlier, struck her attacker Unferth with a large fork. It made balloons go up in his mind. He couldn't see but she poked them and they popped there and lay on the ground.

There was a lot of violence portrayed in the old days, which explains his take. A lot was written about Unferth in the Unforth. She wrote books and he did too. Wealtheow, the wife of the king, published under that name. Whether these other characters wrote depends on the meaning, he thought.

Things were getting a lot more dense, feeling as though time was speeding up. A lot of people thought it was a spoof, but it was more. An unnamed youth, meaning the young man on 118, who read on his bed with his knees raised, looked like a hyper-ventilating Mordred. Maybe he was a prototype. It didn't exactly say what he read, but it was monster food Grendel knew. It was bigger than anything that was made. Super sizing. How do you get the key? Inflation yes, but selection and magnification.

I don't know if it's worth mentioning, but if you blow anything up several times life size you can get one. King Arthur backgrounds it, but it's more than youth rebellion, kids with guns and apples. Graphs pointed back into the book, except there he saw the hand had gotten elliptical. Next to the text's phrase it pointed its finger like a gun and said, "the blessed OOK!"

The door of the H must be into the OoK itself. H, Ook, O, M. There's no time to reveal the other letters, but never look at an Ook. It rhymed his head around like a train blowing little puffs of smoke: Never look in an Ook! Never LOok at an OOk!

He wondered what to do with an Ook? They misspelled it in the monograph, a small point because the sound is the same no matter how you spell it.

The turning point came when he learned that the OoK was the only living being to ever interview his mother.

This is coming under separate cover. But since monsters have by now eaten near half the population everything slowed down. The survivors armed their kids with cell phones and Grendel got online.

Page 156 saw marked in pencil a large star struck in the middle of a storm.
"Star struck, star light, which I might."

The hand was disintegrating. Overstrikes and crossovers, some triangles surfaced under the OoK. He did not look at it.

He *made a decision to turn his will and life over to the care of God.* Leviathan, behemoth did not understand the signs. He did not understand the headless text in his hand.

Part of Document B of the CheesE Blocks

I suggest we adopt our first 95 year old. People in old age reverse childhood, forget what they knew, are and learned, but become beautiful in their innocence and naivete. "If I were you I'd think when someone dies of a sudden illness that it is the same as taking a shower to avoid typhus. The Russians made a music about it. Music means film. In this taking, things mean other than what they mean. If I were you I wouldn't go to the hospital. If I were you I'd drink horse liniment. I'd learn about the ionophore. It's just like the CheesE Blocks. Did you really think I am talking about Mars writing?

Document B attempts to reconstruct the original facsimile in language questionable at some points not only from the dialect, but because the ink was smeared in the transmission requiring a best guess at its meaning.

The Martian stones originally were kept from view because they compromise widely held beliefs of space and government. "Widely" here is an acronym of use. You may wonder how the original writing got carved on Huachuca walls. We all do, but it too is acronym, easy to understand if it bore likenesses to the ancient hand, but the likenesses were only in the mind of the viewer. Somebody has to hide this stuff. There is no need to act like that. We try our best.

They could have been hieroglyphs in tree grains, hidden messages in the erosion of hillsides and in the way leaves fall. None of this either has been conclusively revealed. Suffice it that even were they published, lacking media outcry nothing could have come. They were untitled, meaning, unsung.

So: the writings were passed off as fiction. I assure you this is the furthest from all truth. Even before *CheesE Blocks* was issued on the internet it occurred in quantities so slight as to be rejected by even little mag. Not to say that further efforts made in the startup manufacture of *Blocks* for public consumption at Farmer's Markets and Flea Markets had any other referees than those consumers who bought the *CheesE*. Yes, or no, they did not comprehend. Understanding *CheesE* is not easy, but we're glad to say the label did well. Collectors bought it to display in their private collections. These are untraceable today. This was only an apparent Swiss. Its holes implied a message as a kind of script but it was also an apparent hieroglyph. Not a good choice it turned out.

Two questions remained for our query. Who did translate the original? Who anywhere is competent to read Martian? This is such a problem that computer codes were broken, including the translation, or a version of it, we cannot be sure because it was stolen from NASA vaults where it was secretly kept. We don't know who did this either. Why don't we know so much? Perhaps it was an accident, which is more believable nonsense. Some drunk clerk copied the letters and snuck it out past inspectors, the work uncertifiably scribal by a penciled archivist. Not. No. The observations like an ersatz jazz were probably added just before unconsciousness.

The Disappearance of the NASA Blogs
And Transmission of Its Manuscript States.
Edited from the machine translation of the Japanese of Ovidejo Desuno.

The "intergalactic bridge" stretching between two galaxy clusters 10 million light-years apart has a radio emission connecting these systems. "The electrons, during their radiative life accelerate along the entire filament" when former **NASA** expert **Lola Gulomova** was preparing to turn over to **Russia** information being kept secret by **NASA** related to the "*mysterious unraveling*" of the "*Great Red Spot*" on the planet **Jupiter,** approaching **Earth**, earthquakes are increasing all along the **Western** coasts of **North America**, with **Los Angeles alone recording over 700 of them this past Wednesday**—and **US** military forces this past fortnight having **begun storming beaches of Mars and Washington** in preparations for what they call "*The Big One*" unraveling, which red spot on Jupiter correlated with Mercury's transit of Sol when Lola *subsided.

Introduction

NASA spends millions to hide the discovery and translation of writings they found on Mars.

This is no accident. In their first state those writings indict all of science, but one wonders who in the government knew enough to translate it. Putting that aside, though, we get to the deed of a Martian-Indian-American security guard. Who knows why the lowly clerk grew lax. The stones were stolen.

This tragedy has been compounded over time. However, like those exaggerations that came in the first report from space, the *stones* weren't actually stolen, *they* remained on Mars. Versimilarity!

The facsimiles, or to be exact, facsimiles of the facsimiles were stolen, if you count translations as such. What good would the towering originals do? They wouldn't fit in the Egyptian Room. The scandal arose when these retabulated Martian documents called "stones" ended up in Mexico. How much terrestrializing can we stand? Conjuring petroglyphs, science thinks Mars a potential man!

The best guess is they were carried in the pocket of some clerk. "Have you got it in your pocket?" they will joke in a new age. Maybe it was a janitor. We don't know. He knew nothing of the real discovery but found out that it could make dollar signs. Martian Profit! Over the wall he went and probably drunk. Arrested, hostaged by coyote police, shipped south, was held for ransom. Distraught, he carved Mars' secrets on his cell walls; then he disappeared. The conjectured horror is he was killed.

The next occupant of that cell was one of those taciturn Winnoites who live by the book. He saw the writing on all the wall. They think it their duty to transcribe. This particular Winnoite, a wild escapee from Tampa, had nothing to write on but his lunch. He saved his cheese most days, transcribed the Martian text with the stylus of a pin. Which amazes us only that he should have that much contact with reality. He alleged that according to Mars there is a private issuance into Space for those who obtain the password. Then you may observe the Mars principles like those on earth. He says he learned that life is hostile to itself on Mars where it competes with species in the other Darwin shoe.

Many efforts were made to publish his CheesE text, which revelation, mainly Velveeta, was many times removed from NASA original, except in memory, if you credit its lamentable failings. The message was that earth is endangered by space as much as Mars was made extinct by it. NASA could be put out of business.

Keep in mind the many versions and states in which the writing exists:

1. The Martian original carved on "stones."

2. The NASA translation.

3. The pencil copy made by the purloining clerk.

4. The copy of this written on prison walls.

5. The copy made by the Winnoite on cheese.

6. The cheese slices preserved in his fridge and shown to our narrator who made sketches of the "originals," as here, for the originals were lost when the cheese was eaten.

7. A version of all these in the memory of narrator's account **A**.

8. The translation from Japanese, which came to the narrator in etext from an unknown intermediary source, but for which, nothing could be known of the problem at all.

9. The machine translation of this Japanese from the Etext.

Document **A**, produced below, then comes Document **B**, its reconstruction in modern English.

A)

We reproduce here the A Text:

NASA Blogs

CheesE Blogs released to public view will compromise our space agency government! No wonder that writing carved on Huachuca walls could do what tree grain hieroglyphs, oracle eroded leaves once failed to do. This likeness is only in the mind. Had we published the old one there had been an outcry.

> ***Confidential Memo of The Director to the Deputy Assistant Administrator for Public Affairs*** (DAAPA) NASA

Not true that *CheesE re*published for review. *CheesE* not easy understood. *Blog* crops not *comprehend*. Collector say, "label fable."

What Martian versions translate we don't know. The cracked code was from the vault stole. A clerk snuck south, he shipped for lack of script, next stop cell imprisoned was a Winnowite. Big scrawl peeling he carved Velveeta cheese. Only enough for the text, the labels committed were *memorius*.

That CheesE produce, as rare as any Winnow sketch, better that we, who have eaten much cheese, forget. From descriptions, we digress. Crypt-astronomic sticks out-terrest in space. Space-anglelates the Lunasphere. Stones survive the fifth sphere to compute a species of this Martian text read:

Contact all primitives.
Stones pretext a world.
Psycho regrets, Mars

To stretch that cheese, peel back a slice. Rolled figures of CheesE men create joy.

The great cheese profounder **Logo Hieroglyphs**, in these Swiss notes instructs.

Interested parties study this unbelievable talk. Who ate the CheesE? That's the point. Who believes the written? Pass it off. You live it now but one day will transmit.

We bury paint, photograph thought, give away token opposites, weave poems, ape mind variable texts. Pobres codes!

It'd be better we had got a job. Too late. Go back, remember. We got to go. We got to go with what we got.

To reiterate:

Note: 7. *A version of all this was in the memory of the narrator who wrote Account **A**.*

Note 8. The working of etext in Japanese is as hard to prove as the rest, but were it not for this copy nothing would be known of the problem at all.

*Note 9. **Japan Text: Desuno**: The word desu is the Japanese word for the common form verb, "to be." It is the equivalent of **English** verbs including, "is," "are," and "am. ...** In fact, I and **English*** *cannot be spoken. It is sad... It is writing now using the **translation tool**. Please allow, if the text which cannot be understood.*

B)

Document B reconstructs the facsimile in current language, questionable at some points, not only from the dialect, but ink was sometimes smeared in transmission, requiring a best guess.

CheesE Blocks

The Martian stones were originally kept from view because they compromise widely held beliefs of space agency and government. You may wonder how copies of the original writing got carved on Huachuca walls. We all do. It is easier to understand that they bore likenesses to ancient writing, only however likenesses in the mind of the viewer. They could have been hieroglyphs of the pattern of tree grains, erosion of hillsides and the way leaves fall. None of this was conclusive and frankly not all of it was revealed. Suffice it to say that even were these published, lacking media outcry nothing could come of it.

The writings were passed off as fictions, which I assure you is the furthest thing from the truth. *CheesE Blocks* was issued before the internet, but in a quantity so slight. Further effort at publication was made in startup manufacture of *Blocks* for public consumption. Farmer's Markets, Flea Markets had no peer review, but consumers who bought the *CheesE* did not comprehend. Understanding *CheesE* is not readily achieved, although the label did well. Collectors bought it merely to display in private collections. These are not so easily traced today. The label displayed an apparent Swiss cheese with holes arranged to imply a message. Naturally the language was a kind of English but the script was also an apparent hieroglyphic.

Two questions remained. Who did translate the original? Who anywhere is competent to read Martian? This is unproblematic enough with computer code breaking, but the translation, or a version of it, we cannot be sure, was stolen from NASA vaults where it was secretly kept. We don't know who did this either. Perhaps it was an accident, more believable than conspiracy. Some clerk may have copied the letters and snuck that script out of the building past inspectors. No, the work was not certifiably scribal. It is in pencil, not archival. Observations of an ersatz jazz may have been added before drunkenness.

Not having the original, lack frustrates the detection. This fellow seeking pleasure, probably not knowing what he had, was captured by Mexican police for some offense or other, common enough along the border, and then shipped south for lack of a bribe. Kept incognito in his cell, the next link in the chain turned up, imprisoned for the usual Winnowite fomentations, where the letters were in open view upon cell walls. The metaphor of this is not without appeal, for we all are in various cells, whereupon the persistent translator, lacking paper, carved them on Velveeta Cheese, a block of which was distributed by Red Cross. The writing was labeled on the walls, but those labels were committed to memory, there being only enough cheese for the prime text.

The text itself, *CheesE Blocks*, describes that message better than we can do, even if increasingly rare. The label was part of the discovery process. As to the cheese, much was eaten, but we are not Lamarckian enough to call this is an effective knowledge transfer. How does one get a copy? That Winnowite was a family member who traveled to Central America. His stories and descriptions effected a transfer of data from memory and first-made sketches. These were corrected hesitantly, as though they carried some advice.

Those notebooks retained several pages of facsimiles of facsimiles with the notes from the first NASA thief, and with the benefit of Winnowite observations, comparisons, comments, etc. We regret not having these notes any longer. There were stick figures that opened up the whole sky of crypto-astronomy with its allusions of space and shadow viewed upon projected land forms. You may compare them to Viking maps. *The Mars Shadows* show these well, but satellites do the same. The stones triangulated the allusions. They delved in psychology too, urging a Darwinian premise upon the Lunasphere, which is really no name yet for this penumbra, but the idea both of the stones and itself was that survivals of the fittest best describe earth biology and likewise space. Life forms there are in as much competition as locusts here. Indeed, the stones as they are studied today pretext several other-worldly projects, not to speak of secret societies sprung up. The main illusion, psychologically speaking, concerns autonomy which the stones dismiss as false.

It seems a far reach from such conclusions to the original smooth textured cheese that peeled back revealed more slices in their states. Rolling them in various figures like men, creating whole ply civilizations was founded on no premise other than joy, both for the texture and color of the Orange food. American cheese of the present is not like the original. Studies by the *CheesE* Fund have borne this out. There are stories Yeats was involved.

Imagine the advantages to children posed at an early age who later understood intuitively the nature of all such quests for beauty, personified for them so early. That beauty carried with it a profundity analogous to the hieroglyphs and to the tradition that followed it in the notes, the folklore and instructions of its use. One was somehow both ignorant and privy at the same time.

All our lives we studied the effects and sought to dialogue with interested parties, but where are they? The more we study, the further we go away, the less believed our everyday talk. Our very good mornings are in doubt. Imagine were we to reveal we ourselves once ate the cheese! Who believes so far? Pass it off as satire quaint, but one should entertain familiar truths. You live these things as a child, but one day look up and see the time has come to transmit its knowledge or nothing will survive, we embedded it in paintings and photographs first, but in exhibition the works were mistaken for their opposites. We tried weaving it in poems, aping thought forms of the present day, variable verbal texts that come in posts. We tried writing texts in concrete codes. It had been better if we had just gotten a job. Too late go back to those originals. Too late even remember accurately. We go on with what we've got and this is it.

Note: In a postscript to the first A) text Desuno declared that *he* was not the party who smuggled facsimiles of the Martian translations. Had he done this, he says, then years before, those Mayan hierarchs carved on prison walls, counterfeited on *CheesE Blocks* delivered by Red Cross, would have been known to all.

The Winnowite

We would argue some caveats to the above, which subsequent
compilation is many times removed from the NASA report that had
its own lamentable failings. Was it a fantasy or translation? In any
case the Mars message promoted a notion that earth was as much
endangered by its connection to alien life as Mars had been made
extinct by it. It is a trail long cold. If you've worked for NASA you
have an idea what this is about. Anyway, the authorities observe
Mars protocols on earth like the old men of Pindar's golden age, but
in Martian of course. They go down the palimpsest path from the
equivalence written on tree trunks to the cheese text itself. Oh now
you want to know!

Be human man, accept your fate. Do not kick against the pricks.
Prick ye gads, the goads of gods. God goads sounds a misprint. Gods
with gonads, was written on the blocks. What else was there? For
that sole purpose we stay up late. It involves the Grand Canyon and
the cycle of evaporation. Of course it does, but it is not our purpose
to edit out irrelevancies. You can figure it while you ponder how the
original writing got carved on Huachuca walls. The less said of that
the better, meaning the more. Fort Huachuca is a blind for Oaxaca
and the Ubutu. Everything has a meaning if blind.

Whether the smoking gun is astrolabes, spaceships off the new
planet Mercury, Saturn, Jupiter, finite in number, newly discovered
penal colonies on Mars, lingerers on the dark moon that spark
apocalypse status for earth, if you see things headed in that direction
today remember Jung's mind.

Conversations of revived earth epic get like this. Heaven and earth
we say, and hell. A new literature of the old, Dante writing in code,
Milton taken literally! Goober cheese of ancient cosmology, angels,
spaceships that come and go, can you forgive it? What is so
important about earth that it should attract such ruckus unless it is
the same hunger that preoccupies. Hunger or not, or speculation
about the glucose cycle and addiction, we read back from the literal
the divine, although the divine is not any more than the folks who
get stoned in Peru to penetrate the outer layer with idols of the past,

wood and stone, cloth vested with belief as real. What it is that believing makes so? Enlightenment? There is no enlightenment. The amulets and talismans, good thoughts directed to the sylphs and in the next breath actors and scientists argue immortality from trapezoids. Politicians secretly hide their agenda in cheese! In cheese you can buy at the store, mind you, bring home and put in the cold drawer. Cheese you can melt on toast like occultists organize the planet and governments orchestrate big dreama! Roll cheese. Take one.

Here is an acronym of history become epic poetry, the past in the present of boats off their moorings adrift. the lead time however prevents realization. That's why we have the cheese. Hurry to get the news before, which to tell: the Pope contacted by ET, the Space Agency, Noam Chomsky, martial law, currency devalued, sun spots, asteroids, eclipses, even *The Planet Formerly Known as Earth* folded before its planned demise. Does cheese narrate crowned gods who rule in their stead? What happened to all the men? If there was ever a time for giant killers to come…. not inflated reputations and media interviews: NASA's new T-shirt. MIT renames their library, A New Center for Alums in New York misspelled. There is no need to act like that. Somebody has to hide this stuff. We try our best.

The stones weren't stolen. They're still on Mars. What good would 50,000 foot originals be? Not even the British Museum transports batholiths. Facsimiles were stolen and the translations as such. The scandal arose when retabulated Martian documents, called "stones," ended up in Mexico. How much can you stand?

Each pixel in the original was a multi-spectral image, with Profit with the Martian autofluoresced on the cover. That secret prospectus conjured that petroglyphs of a Synchrotron light, proposed Mars as a potential earth. I kid you not, they sent probes for water. They'd have better luck finding life in a pea, but a best guess has the translation carried out in the pocket of a clerk. One thing's sure, the purloiner knew social networks, at least until NASA squelched it and remarketed the thing to private industry.. How do we know? There were many leaks. We pulled the usual investigative blinds. Over the wall uncelebrated and drunk, arrested by police and shipped south, thus were carved Mars' secrets on the jailhouse wall.

NASA spent millions to hide the discovery and translation because, as said, those writings implicate all science. The cover up was no accident. One wonders who in government knew enough to translate Martian metadata mined through fluorescence astronomy. Putting that aside we get some lowly American clerk who stole it. It was an inside job.

It is a trail long cold. The next occupant of that cell was one of those taciturn Winnowite, who lived by the book-- if you don't know their ways, they're as alien to earth as Mars-- when the Winnowite saw the writing on the wall he thought it was a Text. These people are nuts for Text. We capitalize to show that Winnowites think it their duty to *transcribe* reality, which they say exists in every rock, man, plant, branch, tree. Transcribe it for what? It is a peculiar poetry.

This Winnowite, escaped from Tampa from one of their own prison farms, was held prisoner in that jail long enough for the Bond to wear off. This gets some sympathy. The Bond itself is not easily known. We must illumine it, except of course, as you know, we do not believe in illumination any more than we do in enlightenment. He wrote the writing down, saved his cheese day after day until he had transcribed in earnest the much abused Munchhausen text with a pin. With nothing to write on but his lunch, it amazes me he had so much. According to *The Mars Report* this resulted in a private issuance of Space credentials to him, indeed to all who obtain the password like he did. If you've never worked for NASA you have no idea what this is about. Anyway, the authorities began to observe the Mars protocols on earth like the old men of the golden age in Pindar. They go down the path of the Archimedes Palimpsest, but in Martian of course, from the equivalence written on tree trunks in their center to the cheese text itself. Oh *now* you want to know!

Whether the smoking gun is astrolabes, spaceships off the new planet Mercury, Saturn, Jupiter, finite in number, newly discovered penal colonies on Mars, lingerers on the dark moon spark apocalypse status for earth. We know nothing without a sense of pride in this fictional acceptance and a seat at the table, names, lights. So the revelations of cheese amount to this, and chimeras go up in fumes emanating from cheese. You say the cheese has more holes than not. Half empty, half full. Look closely at the craters, what once was known as *nihil cognentesis solipsis is no metaverse any more than* a million less important things like chemtrails or Monarch children, artificial life forms cloned from bits of bone, halving Earth's pop to make it seem natural, all which intolerant Wigamites on a near campus can be spotted in their wind socks.

Why not just memorialze the thing, you say. Well he did that, our Winnowite; the cheese was an important confirmation of his memory. Even had the initial purloining clerk not passed to the Winnowite these remains, the transmission of the text released by authorities could not be traced back to him. The Winnowite went back to his old path. The Martian writings were published in Tampa by the Winnowite Press. Called *CheesE Blocks*, it is today available only in reissue, in the main a Velveeta, but there is also a Gouda, among others. This subsequent compilation is many times removed from NASA report, which had its own lamentable failings.

Legends of the Fall

I have no idea what this is about but I enjoyed reading it and would like to post it because posting it is why I started this freakin' site anyway. But I'd like to ask you to maybe try to shorten it a little from about midway through till the end? It's maybe a little too long, or maybe my pleasureable incomprehension only could hang so long, and therefore my editorial instinct is to ask you to limit the part that made me zone out a bit, ok? If so, if you send a quick revision, I'll post it real, real soon, like tomorrow. Also, give me a link to embed in your name, like to something else you've written etc. Anyway - thanks again for sending more stuff, and sending stuff that's sort of wonderfully baffling. Lee Klein, *Eyeshot*.

Poemato is a source of poemate power,
foundation of our next world home.
We are all going to live in poems.
Giant poematoes built on carbon stands
will be planted on sea and land.
This organ is sure to work for flesh
to bear the brunt of the poemate seed
in the mind- felled man.
That soul will delve roots.
BuckaFeller himself approved the site.
We go back to begin this phenom.

Anyway, that's the pitch. Poemato lets fly. Profanations of our joy. These days we blame the pigocerous for turning the lewd sacred, not that which is, but that which cannot be.

They all say flesh is grass, that it fades like the flower and then comes the mower, but mass mind makes a way in telecom. It's the difference between the poemato and the nut. The think glands are like walnuts. Weverboy's walking around with nuts inside. He get too big we shrink'em. Too small we give supplements. Snapdragons and poultry and all gliding rhythms of periodicity look like McDonalds, just one pizza and all else a copy and so on with robber plots and toe holds. We whitewash the words and put sun cream on the trunks.

Detasseled poems benefit these thin-skinned heads. That's why the poemato has changed where it made its vulgar bed. Weep for this poemato cut from air amid the blaze of noon, but there is still a poemato moon. Also there's chanting now in front of city jail:

"The Bourbons, what did they use for tools, huh, huh, what did they use for tools?"
It's a question of physic.
"How do you know huh?"
The answer is as problematic as a river of light that flows through every living thing.

In this context we should add, but it may be obvious, that the Igods had iridescent coats, feathers that would molt from heads and pomegranates that fluttered down at night like wingy batgans and poms.

"But if that is so obvious why has the garden become extinct?"

Consider this yourselves when you believe what is Newtonicly cast on iPod, living close to the heart that hands made with new powers.

"Hey baby! Is this a spiritual world?"

It was the one paradise thorn that trapped the man and suspended his license, pecked down beaks in earth and pulled up another poetatum. We would all get vaccinated for it, live happily after, but for the bodies of flesh, the desiccated death and winter of the nonseasonal man. Now you need to get a license to love the poemato, the three syllable fruit.

"Where have all the bodies gone?"

These things mattered to the thistle thane, the gray green boundary down which rivers flew to the great hymned being lost.

PANCAKE Syntazz

From planting to milk stage when planted at the summer monsoon in our region it produces larger ears but takes longer. This fresh green roasted over mesquite coals and sun-dried on the cob can be shelled and made into Huun Hahk Chu'i (corn pinole) or Ga'ivsa, stone ground. Roasting gives the kernels a sweet taste and a hard texture that shatters when cracked. Cooked Ga'ivsa has more

*body, and a texture like risotto. Huun Hahk Chu'i and Ga'ivsa have
an exceptional sweetness.*

"Get hold of them electric lights, make ads." Nothing
Christmas cannot be changed opposite!
"In the smelter the solid runs."
Recase the solid unsolid god of the age, ePANCAKE!
Good to eat and good for you each morning.

Making way for telecom products, themselves virtually
human, needs no labels or lapels to buttonhole. Ordain the
identification.

Jo Pan spoke the eloquent marvels of podcasting the
familiar to the divine. "You can do it too," he urged the
mannequin children who worked through the boxed
syntax of Syntazz.

You remember Syn? Syn was lost when Pancake rescued
her from Dragon. Joe Pan flew down in his marvel wave
machine and killed the bad and returned her home nice to mom.

Rip Law was another character in the Pancake Empire.
In later T shirts he escaped and had a black mask, oh Ignatius!

His schemes were manifold. Not that they touched flesh
that ate raw food or played among the rocks tracking lizards,
followed bee lines to water or stalked deer in a friendly manner.
That's how to learn to hunt, to hunt. To be still, be silent. To be
invisible, what won't come to such a one!

So Johnny Cake ran.
Outran every other.
Johnny Cake was Pan Cake
who was like Rip Law
who was like IGod
and he ran and ran and he ran.

He got himself out of oven town. He got himself up-pulled, fup, by his straps. He could have been American. He won a gold medal. It was just that simple. He said, "I think I can." He out ran his brother, his parents, the work doers, the wolf and the bear but the fox, that lousy fox waited.

"Here is a world where everybody is disproving themselves," was Flesh's discovery of the spirit world. The spirit world was the physical world inhabited by the people opposed to the physical world inhabited by animals and plants.

Things make sense if you just turn them upside down.

People were carrying around the spirit inside and it was spoiling the outside. Physically they were good red meat and blood and bone and that could easily go thump.
And that was all right. Like animals.

But spiritually it was another case, stuffed with rags and cotton and had shoe button eyes, which is why they couldn't see the sequence of action. Little rag heads thought they were in a soda water ghetto afraid of being made into soup, all soft and loppy and full of cotton and not empty at all or hollow like someone had said.

Course what is cotton but filler and you could as easy use corn shucks or stuffing, straw man or batting, just anything to fill a void.

So spiritually they really didn't work and needed fill.

They were stuffed stuffing and wadding and packing and when you unwrapped the shell there was nothing in it at all but packing.

The only explanation anybody ever gave for this was that they fell through a hole or what and ended up here in this land. That was the extent of their spiritual wasold.

Universally there used to be an outside and an in, an up and down, now there was only an in. The kingdom heaved on the banks but without there was faeries and boloins, fiction and faction.

"The great still pressed bird song and orange count cobbled to a hoax."
If you're flesh out to save the button you care about such.

Thee was not.
Thee didn't mean to do it.
Thee was pushed.
That evil had about decided thee wasn't much since thee never did nanny thing that it could see. This vastly opaque style of life.

There is no time to go into what that life consists of, but evil could see into the little ragherds since it had also planned the rag hearts.

"Yes take it for granted that there are spiritual organs, counterparts to the physical, some more notable than others. The spirit liver. The circumcision of the heart."

What does our flesh do with that?
Male vestiges of feminine spirit.
Reflections through a dark flask.

Have you ever yourselves a peek of the naked heart? Leave it in the pericard, hangin' on the rack? The heart reclothed in a T- shirt with a slogan blessed. *Once circumcised fears the fire.*

Hide, hide it don't you think? The truth is exposed .
Clothe the heart?

"The shadow of the might" said Pearl. It will cover me
with fathers. Cut then cover. Cut the fat, cut the sweet. Purify by
blood not work.

"Who is your tailor?"
I buy the rack.

There is a grain of camphor for the poor in the notion
that the first shall be last. Look what happened to Lazarus.

Somewhere exists the idea of just. But they say God looks
on the heart.

The post delivers mostly bills, junk mail and only once a
year that check.

"Shall I do evil that good may come?"
That is the flesh question, thinking the cowman to
murder.

"But did not the Aposty say he wished himself cursed for
the people, poetically quoting those who ask to be a killed in
place of the people?"

The pleoplle always the poeop-ple, take all evil upon him
that good may come. The serpent as the most subtile beast
virtually formed the native plant society for his purposes.
Preserve the Prairie. What org not infiltrated with cunning?

The good was evil the evil was good.
The cow and its could.
The boy in the hood.
Dead meat of food.
Is a burger spiritual outside the meat?
To such uses high mind is put.
Hunt a really good spiritual.
A smell of earth burger.

A cockcrow bourger.
No chicken patty slice of pungent air,
a burger that will satisfy till tummy rocks,
cactus flower and affection,
light sprinkled gobbets of sun,
alchemy dawn. Swell tin place.
A brink of a burger spiritually speak.
The bourgner the burgher, the burfger, buffgeefer meat.
I told you spirit worlds ruin the physical!

What to do? The kingdom's within.
All the machinations man continue.
 But the evil is good. Good economy. Good evolution.
Good psychology. Without evil. Boring. So be glad the
evilisgood. What did you expect?

Whow could he do it to me? Assuming he did.
Picking the wings off flies. Rototiling the ear.
"Why he do it?"
"What the charge?"
 "You did yourself you bleeding nainny!" Turned
opposite. Ever yourselves peek at the naked heart?

"But could he be the boy next door?" No, lawlessness is
next door. What else can you say of them when they don't rake
or plow their lawn or even if they do?

Man make up your mind. Spirit or flesh?
"What If the end comes and I don't feel like it?"
He upulled himsle fup by his own boot straps.
He could have been amermican.
He won a gold medal.
It was just that silmple. He sadi "I thilnk I can, I knew I
could."
He outsran his mbrother, hils parents, the workders, the
woldf and the fbear but fowx was wailting.

Rehoboth Starr

These are 39 canonical stories. All but one (Rehoboth Starr) published. You can read the first seven online. The first question is: What is The JFK Order, but you already know! Think about it. Look up "dome" under search at the site. More questions as we go. It is a world view in vitrio. These stories are not going to disappoint. They are full of true insights into the nature of things, which is, what it is to not be, not be simultaneously.

"Eagin, I can't publish this story of Rheb's as it stands and it's way too much trouble for her if it's true the way she tells it. Maybe you turn it into a mystery."

"Well I never wrote a mystery Bob."

"Don't start, she's enough. I read you Eagin Arthur. I guess you're fanciful enough."

"Well what's the mystery then."
"Rheb, what's the mystery?"
"It's not a mystery. It's a history."

"Well how about you call the newspaper Rheb and give it to the purple shirts."
"Come on Uncle Bob, I pack horses and give trail rides."
"Sure, ok, but we would not want the setting to be the whole Grand Canyon and it sounds to me like a blood bath. What are you Shakespeare? You're the only one to return?"

"What can I say, that's what happened."

"If that's what happened, where are the police reports?"

"Where were the police reports when you were in Argentina Uncle Bob?"

"Cute Rheb, but is it fiction or fact, make up your mind. If fact and there's no police reports then the spooks are going to want you to disappear. If this national security thing is fact then you're in for a world of hurt, but call it a mystery, embellish it, Eagin's middle name, and we can say whatever we want."

"What's this national bloodbath? In the Grand Canyon. Hey Bob I can play pandemonium on that. How 'bout a punctured strata redirects the river, an ecological suspension of the mythical causes riots in cities by irate Indians led by Alexie. Whee. Upset the balance, tilt the poles."

"I think your pole already tilted Eagin."

"Wait, I can do better. Are they crazies or money grubbers, who align the poles to bring in the new age? Demented or deceived? See Bob, I do journalism. Headline: Scientific backing behind the scenes pits the tetrahedral adherents of a low ceilinged prairie style against the space agency in the redesign of a Grand Canyon, a Dome as precursor for protected earth. WW III held in the Gran Can. Or purple in this: New Age Bowl Game Turned To a Lake."

"Help Uncle Bob, it hurts already. Is this the world of hurt you promised me? Who is this guy?"
"Eagin Arthur, he escaped from a think tank Rheb."

"Look, I'll show you, I can do mystery:

Dateline: Williams, Arizona. Power companies deregulate the flow from Lake Powell, increase power. **Transportation to secret government projects in the Grand Canyon masked by tourist over flights.** Hey I can even do fantasy: *Levitate the Grand Canyon to another spot. Put in electrodes and just leave a hole in the ground.* Who would notice? *Steal the Grand Canyon, hold it for ransom.* I guess that's satire. Come genres one and all."

"See Rheb he's a perfect imbalance."
"Eagin I think you're fun."

"She thinks you're nuts."

"Jus' trying to help."

"Look Rheb why don't you tell him how it started, then we'll see."

"Well, like all folk that long to go on pilgrimage, *when that April in showers sweet…*

"Bob, she's pullin' our leg."

"Rheb, you've been hitchhiking."

"Yes Uncle Bob."

"Well all's I know to try is for you and Eagin to get me some chapters to look at. You tell him the story and Eagin you put some of your wild flowers in it now, ya' hear?"

Ailin Penlight

We feel that the allusive language play of your piece provides myriad avenues for response, and we'd like to includethe attached excerpted version to the Post-Hole project if that's alright with you. We feel the that the piece as submitted loses momentum toward the end, and that the sense of closure evoked in this excerpted version strengthens the piece and opens it to interconnection with other pieces we have on the site.

Jack Bommb shook the light from his wife's hand.
She used to read maps with it at night.
 He bellowed like a conductor on a train and threw it at the Grand Canyon.

Here's where that munchkin light could boast, "I think I can, I can," and orbit El Tovar in space, an *E. Pluribus Unum* for all to see their source, go round like the dish like a satellite before the mother ship could take a lumpen home.

That night our Wal-Mart whirled its beacon to the lost.
"Come buy, come buy," the omnivore said,
"come, lay your pence upon my staring lidless eye."

Jack Bomb, country ham, whistled his stops again.
"LOOK OUT BELOW," he cried.
It did no good to win him mention except by dispatch to 211.

***

Ecomen come and go in space.
Shoemaker's ashes are on the moon and Tombaugh soon will play
the slots beyond 'Ptune.
But the essence of return is to connect, for when that Taiwan lady
pricks the web, a woof erupts on earth.

Who is she?
 Has she got a penlight?

Good news friends, directions on the box show how to do your part,
connect your flight.

"Do your part to shoot the moon," it says:
"extend rudder as clip, catch drift."

But malfunction forced that prop upon a ridge.
 It bounced off a stone like a dodo egg and lay staring in the dark.

***

Only connect, connect, connect, only connect and connect.
The train rolled over the railroad track oblivious to the connecting
crack, it did not look out below. And those below did not look up.
They had not read the wind.

Leo opened to the coming poem.
Round that fire Dag conversed his flask.
Cowgirl Lipsy imagined herself a bath.
Mr. Partridge piled dirt between his feet.

Another plied a tune upon a boot.
The wind chats fidgeted as the zodiac devolved.
More dark came.

***

Imagine we're talking dodo egg here not Einstein.
Dodo however can read.
Dodo got egg look, but he got the book even if he be stone.
Penlight meets rock.
They did not see the rock collide.

Slowly surface slid to air.
Inertia, that once failed Zen, transferred.

All things must fall but one thing moves the king. Le Roi!
The light lay stunned, but the stone egg sailed.
Long live the King!

The little Lady of Taiwan got out her bag and ground powder for her nose.

***

Down, down dodo fell to Leo's song.
It would have smashed him in the nose had he not bent over for coffee.
That stone knew more of land than Voyager did.
 It sang a song of glory.
A stone upon a mountain's chance of flight? Slim to none.

When did that astronaut see earth grow big?
 It is a trick of consciousness that hits our heads.
 Not gently into night, it came with fire, sailed past Leo's shoulder and hit the saucepan square.

This black hole flipped quark on Lipsey's front which stream
Newtonicly transferred to mouth.

She could both chew and smoke.

Tobacco sauce shot straight in TidB's eyes while the saucepan clanged below.
The rock then landed in a bed of coals.

Children appreciate it.
Sparks came down.

Dark screams roused mules who saw their burdens dismount.
These words have pictures if you can believe.

The sparks are falling.
The mules are bawling.
TidB is waving blind.

Good students fell in three directions. The coals took buggies to the west while Phoenix scalped the Patagon beneath.

Did Jack Bommb pay the bill? There is no Jack Bommb in the book.

***

We could send down a platitude. The locale party space could attach it to a rock.
"Better the trouble already caused than not."

How 'bout abstractly, "a response to your request has now been served?"
Injections, a pill, a line from Milton might work.

But in that contest TidB would come in first.
Nicotania liquida caught him full in the face, caused him to blurt.
"Water," he shouted, just before the fire, "water, water, water."

Prophylaxis tapped the skillet.
But give Lipsy credit for TidB's finish and also one of her own.

Sparks in her hair induced a moose-like shriek one octave up as the graduate students fell and disappeared two feet down.

The beat goes like this:

> water, water,
> tap, tip, top,
> eeeeaaaggghh! eeeeaaaggghh!
> thump, thump, thump.

That breaker of stallions, ardent Leo, was a quick-draw too.
With a mug full of coffee he dowsed Lipsy's hair.
Add therefore "splat," for the coffee was cold.

That was the Quixote conference where mules stamped and the Boombay Indian scout stared, when Leo announced himself, "a light, a light, nobody move!"

***

Up on the precipice that light heard Leo's call. Recent transfers have no roots at all.

Its motion sawed the noonosphere.

Light pushed air, the physics is explained, the weary migrant from Jack Bommb's world slid down to Leo's cry.

Normally a cataclysm of events must follow in the trail.
Normally after we inquire of light, miniatures are discovered in the alien cause.
Then we are bound to ask then, how do you know these lights originate on Mother Earth?
How do you know they are not a televised race or maybe the invention of NASA itself?

The joy of inquiry can never be fulfilled.
How can you know the cyber-self did not evolve in the desiccate found only in Grand Canyon?

A modern scientist, the great Horace Lamb, is examining our requests.

He said that when Lowell discovered the Ice Planets anything was allowed.

We are looking for more brief and powerful pulses.

Overflights
From the Desk of Pedro Escadero

Pedro Escadero is a Science Advisory Board Member and Chairman of Speleology at Southwest Cave Conservation, a branch of The Carl Sagan SETI Institute, a Coyote Center of the Esner Foundation. He was a presiding myth hat at the Anthropos of Geneva. Many long and mazy studies of volumetric cave bone data and traditional agave vacuñas, guanacos, llamas, alpacas, salt caves and caverns help explain why these caves are mostly named for women, which alcoves and emplacement strategies predict and detect analogue caves on Mars from these sites enter the world of Overflights. Subsurface cavities via thermal infrared remote sensing to determine cave volume from the thermal signal strength have appeared in his Old Ice Eel articles in El Pais and Der Spiegel.

I am Pedro Escadero.

As chief *escritoire, psicologo*, and *proscribere* to Parks and Wildlife, I explain canyon psychology upon its victims. How else can science be known? I probe the down and dark patterns of Mather Point. Aspects of my reporting have been subjective in recent years.

First, it is in nature that things must fall. A pedestrian who speeds up Meteor
Crater will fall to a vertigo of wrong conclusions. A precursor of wrongs, this

doo-wap summons all our tribe upon the verge. Were the Canyon to
cry out, what
would it say, the rocks unpaved?

But before the answer, uniformed firemen race down in blue.
They dismount trucks, descend like shadows on ropes.

Our analysis, this metaphor, forthcoming.
Please do not ignore.
We shall explain the impulse verge.
We prove that She alone, third feminine, recusant female,
gave psyche to our canyon. Remember that projection.

But He whose reputation has suffered, whom you think a bifurcate of
all
that lives, a masculine odor, reflects the tide of night and day.

Thus the impulse both transfers, projects.
It is twice soulful and full of grief, that bottom, *sin fondo*.

Of course we do not think she feels good pulling down. Down and
down.
Sure we get paid for it.
He mirrors those rides, flights beyond price, whose drops of fun
from
treetops took a letting go.

This caused the paradox of which we speak: THE CRISIS IS
THE
LETTING GO..

The apogee first pulls you down. Then in the flow, the range
of motion,
what signs, counselors upon the way, alert us to let go, let go?

Alas, such trails erode a wink. In the world to come it is too
late to say
they fire back up. They shrink with each atrocious fling.

We summon geology to explain, order the assumptions.
Affirm what all have come to know, what mountains see, the fall of
rocks to sand.
That sand, particulate, is our triumvirand!

So turning poleless we know it feels. WE FALL TO SEE IF WE
CAN DO IT, to survive the trouble we have caused.

This is understood by the Empathy Boys who rush themselves to the
brink and over.
This is understood by our government.

How else explain the public haste to wily fact?
It is Neolithic turf up there behind Hopi House. They tee up and
drive out.

So in the parlance of the matter we get down to science.
Our research shows the canyon rims portend a kiss.
The canyon is half lip, the bottom.
The "rims" above must seek the schists, the teeth submerged in
magma red.

Seeker on edge feels this the more, works in quandary to position,
for who but he should marry that wide pose with sky?

How does it feel for such dim psych when sky lips tread the beams
of rock? Jealousy is just like art. We can fly, transport. We rock.

That is what they think, but failing lift dismount the rocks.
And light pours down, the long way down Colorado . From the burst
of pithy navel to the reach of her long loins. There is no surviving.
The good that comes from this is now applied from nursery rhymes
to Keats. But how many have heeded?

I wanted
an eider down puff
for my dolly
of very soft stuff.

But turn a moment from this pathos, souls. What of those millions,
who come to edge themselves? Why has no Park Servant, harness
tied, jerked back, forever to suborn the edge, *recuerdo de memoria*!
where silence in the ears is consolation, but a living tear?

"Purest of heart! Thou need'st not ask of me
What this strong music in the soul may be!"
How can they ask? What gratitude from *desconsolado*, the failed
Parks pilgrim returned to every day, mere bubble at the brim? *Pero
que inaprecio de mismos lastima*!

So take into the air one quiet breath and let it out.
That is a help for pain.

Thanks now to the government which licensed this estudio.
That much remains the same.
Thanks to all the patient insights offered heathen.
 Come down and hear us at El Tovar this season.
 For then we shall be truly one.

The world will lie before us as a land of dreams.

A Spiritual Tour of Grand Canyon

We stopped for night. An hour to dark. No tents, "see the
night sky of your dreams."
We blew up their pads, threw down the dudes, got out stools,
made fire on transported logs. Presto. Sandwiches.

Wouldn't you love to be a transported log?
In this business you get along with authorities.
No fire on the trail.
No camping outside a campground.
We dumped the dudes on the ground at dark.

I right then didn't need an omen. A golf ball hit high up, ricocheted down. Which told me something.

Some fool was teeing off.

Nobody even saw it.

Time speeds up and slows down when you leave the rim.

Dudes gathered at the fire. Leo threw an icebreaker. I almost said id breaker.

He asked if they thought anything had changed.

In two hours!

Rebots looked at his hands, turned pale and sat down. Said he had, I'm quoting, "stars on the mount of Mercury but they were gone."

TidB at that moment grew black wires out his nose.

Kidding!

The book guy, Paul Polymer apropos of nothing, twitching and tapping, said he hated books.

I'm thinking he's on medication.

Said he's going to leave a donation at the Shrine of Printing.

Laura Dobson, nicknamed "Happy," a professor, told her wilderness credo, "all that is spiritual mimics the divine."

Then she looked at Rebots and cried, "shrive me, shrive me, spirit man."

Spirits and its and its.

Leo had them sit on rocks and stools by the fire. He was going to give the lesson. I doubt he had a license for anything. From that late start we weren't half down, out from back rock only in feet.

"Of course the Redman projected his reality on the pseudo-sphere.

Because we are alive we make it alive.

Animism is our good wish to the stone.
Live, we say, like us.
But the stone won't say that to us.
If it did talk we wouldn't like what it said.
Matter has contempt for spirit, even while spirit coaxes the least imagined life from it. That's our paradox. We're both."

This was the old Indian of the heart routine. Nobody comes out west without his Indian. Maybe the mule buster will sign autographs.

The buster had skin like toast, a red kerchief around his throat.
His mule had an omega brand upside down on the rump.
Said his name was Chee Dom Bombay.

Leo kept going.

"Consider what we see as surface open and obvious.
Moralists call what is evil underneath.
A dark evil with a red face or a red evil with a black face.
Red, white and black are the three colors of earth that the dualism of matter frightens into submission.
Naturalists apprehend the under bird, the inner rock.
In the words of the poet, 'what has no arms, no legs, no skin, no teeth?'"

I wanted to raise my hand, "fried egg," but it has skin.
A bucket of grits has teeth.
But oh the urge to pee!
I didn't say that.

"The days of participation mystique are over.
We no longer think to join with nature. Nature joins with us.
We open a dialogue with the natural world. Communicate the in and out.
Self fulfillment in us is realization for the grass.
We open a road, at first a toll road, between nature and man. Sorry, human beings.

We must be silent to hear forces sweeping the grasslands, spirit fires.
 We must learn to smell again, renew the nose within.
 When we talk we cannot hear.
 So be silent my friends and feel the inner canyon."

Tell the sun to stand still!

The sun was gone.
 Masses of shoulders and heads looked down.
 The rock giants were hoping for pigmy talk.

I listened to the heart-steady pressure of blood in my ears. The rocks come apart. Tree roots of weather splits. Three minutes and they pray for a phone, five and they start a rockslide.

The fire cracked. A shifting of positions. Switchboards lit up.

If I see any spirit fires starting I'm gonna squirt.
 Were they holding their breath?
 Then Partridge started in neat.

"The charm of Taliesin is the great concrete roof overhead, the kiva atmosphere. Like a meeting of elders.
 I remember Dr. Wright built all his doorways low because he was short, as if you needed to believe in him before you entered his temple or otherwise the whole thing would crash in on your head.
 Not that Frank Lloyd Wright thought himself a god, but it's no place to be claustrophobic.
 Wasn't he modeling this Grand Canyon and its thighs, extending and sealing them over with beams of reinforced cement, leaving two or three doors at the heads of the trails.
 A solid dome.
 We could be down here spelunking with lanterns and breathing humid air."

The inner canyon swallowed.

Leo waved his arm at me.

"Come on over to the fire Rheb so we can get to know you."

I waved back but got off the hook when Happy Dobson caught the ball.

"Blake thought the same, not about the Canyon but about the eternal man that he said was flesh bound because he manufactured an idea of himself like girders and beams, a metaphysical stone imprisoned with a really low roof of cruelty.

So it was into a canyon they fell.

That's a lot like covering over this place or paving in the sky or prairie.

Maybe Wright's house for troglodyte heads creaks and shifts with every foundation!

Then the beautiful god of Shelley with his clear limbs and skin would be no more.

The piety of sky would be a misshapen darkness."

What was in those sandwiches?

Down and down she goes and where she stops nobody knows.

I will absolutely get right over to that fire.

Nobody seemed to notice she was talking funny.

I call it first night dudisms.

They calm down later usually.

But it's like they have to one up.

Then bookman TidB went off.

"I know what you mean. This place is spooky, but red kachinas and fallen skies aren't the danger. The danger is rocks and cliffs and snakes and pits.

Any time you get off paved roads people spend days waiting to get rescued even in the helicopter age. Sure they get saved. But it maxes out the plastic. Their wallets are as dry as their throats.

You think they ever come back here? What's the saying,
"once dreaded biers the pyre?"
     They run fast, jump the fence and hide in buildings and
parks the rest of their life.
     Maybe they come out to mow a lawn or clip a hedge, but
they're back in fast, head for shadows of curtains in rooms.

     You know what they'd say to the rest of us don't you?
  Go back! Go back!"

"Yo, Tidbetter," Leo called.

Too much silence is not a good think, to say it the way
Happy talked.

For me the stars are sparking oval V's and Semitic alphabets
that spell the word nobody can pronounce.
     You never get it, but on good nights try to wrap the thing. I'd
rather a restoration than a demolition of those constellations in
dreams that don't exist.
     The highest and the lowest and the in between.

Partridge, who had started it all looked pretty comfortable
now, stretched his feet toward the fire.
     The soles of his boots were smoking.
     Then he started to smile.

"I've just returned from a conference on inner fears.
     A lot of it seems to come from our guilt at having ignored the
beauty of the world.
     Everywhere we go we carry our associations, habits of being
passed down long ago, the whole gold cart of our culture.
     It's like a comet's tail invisible to the eye, but not to the
conscience.
     The *original pot is our idea*, but we pass through a world of
broken shards, fragments we piece together.
     But what does it all amount to but dust.
     Those little spider webs on the ground near the trail? They're
supposed to catch bugs but they catch a lot more dust.

And of course the bugs turn to dust.

Satellite dishes are like spider webs.

Their programs are dust.

Our problem is what to do about all the dust, or to bring it back to conscience, what to do with all the fear and the guilt.

Is dust worthy of contrition on our part.

As Leo was saying, we're matter and spirit. Matter is dust. What is spirit, the sun?

And as Mr.TidB suggests, the sun can bake your blood in a Petri dish.

There must be an earth to the spirit though because greed boils down to dust.

Pride dries up to dust, that dust settled by squirrels, shadowed by ravens.

We shadow the spirit like a dark entrance to caves where once dwelt the art of that age."

A monologue.

"And not one of us is holding still till we get a grip.

The canyon gets deeper, the shards get smaller.

Axes, pots and pahoes are all that's left.

In payment for it we have the artifice of our lives, like master Dedalus, and with him a dream ticket to the earth navel."

This was one doozie of a dude.

Who ever heard anything like it?

But he warmed up even from there.

"So are we to apologize to the dust for our being?

Are we to say that earth is sacred, life is holy, leaves are holy?

Are you holy?"

Holy moly, holy moly.

"Can you join us in our worship, we who worry about the destruction of species, for the dust that leaves no trace?

It is the universal cry.
The rocks, stones and trees cry out for dust much like
martyrs, much like logs cry out for trucks."

Oh the call of the log!
I have heard it often.

"So how shall we deal with the contradiction of ourselves?
Shall we go to an act of contrition or to timber sales.
Shall we deny it, things getting better.
Sacred or profane the flesh, the forest, or neither?
The oak, pine, lake spring worlds of the natural man need a
metaphysic, a way out of this or that, that or this dust."

Not just a doozie.
A whoozie doozie.

"So the great poets and thinkers call for exploration of
spiritual worlds.
As the great author of *Tuttle Inland* says, log truck drivers
rise earlier than the students of Zen.
Log drivers have a life, a vocation, a Zen, but tourists merely
fun.
They sit Zen at 5 am. Then they don't sit.
Garbage truck drivers sit all day."

I got it.

Garbage truckers sit to work.
Zen tourists work to sit.
Work means worship.
Eat dust, think dust, love dust.

"Leo and I are one in this. Not that two are one, but two in
one, dust and spirit, matter and energy.
To resolve the conflict, animate stone, put wind in the rock,
that is your work upon yourself while the log truck is driving, to
resolve the contradictions."

After you gas them, the gophers come out and you slit their throat.

What's in it for him to talk that way?
 I wondered if they noticed how he broke down at the end.

It looked like they had all fainted.
I thought I was gonna have to give first aid.
The only one who looked untouched was the husband of
Happy Dobbs who had a wide grin on his face and threw still more
wood on the fire.

"Well you know Professor I've a theory about all of that.
I call it the technological suspension of the mythical.
We're going to invent these new ways and use them, just
cause we can.
Might makes right. Mill said so. His father beat him so he
learned Latin.
He beat him again and he learned Greek.
Beat your dog. I call it utility Shakespeare.
 A little humanity at college.
Yes. Might and Right. And sight.
When did we ever invent anything we didn't use?
Spare body parts are close at hand.
I don't mean you sweetheart," he said, turning to his wife.
"Just manufacture fetal tissue."

The five graduate students had mounted different parts of the
same rock. They hung off into space in several directions. They were
boys of their time, hair both struck straight up and out, sort of like a
perm of the Imo Jima flag raising.

Lipsy teased them.
"Yawl look like Imo Jima!
How can ya ride a mule all day and get off to ride that rock
all night.
 I know I'm not made of stone."

She wiggled and spat in the fire from the chaw in her mouth,
"this here'll settle that dust.

Now Leo, didn't cha promise to tell us about the wild west and such?"

"Well which stories do you want to hear? Indian stories, settler stories, nature stories…"

"Tell us that one you did in Sedona, you know, Ai-oo, that coyote thing."

There's nothing like dudes kicked back.

The mules had no fire. They were tended by the buster, just far enough off to prevent most of the smell.
Caught between the odor and the gas, I'm seeking the middle ground.

It sounded like the buster was teaching the mules German.
Pigish saucers of *umlaut* floated over the fire where it looked like Leo and Rebots were getting ready to pop the really biggo question, something like, "is the Boombay Indian primitive the thought stream none can enter?"

Hippie Polymer was playin' Crosby, Stills and Diddley, tapping his foot in a sway.
He had given out a hot list at the trailhead:

Trotsky's *Life of Lenin*. First English. Signed by Solzhenitsyn in Cyrillic. Mint. 2500.
Picasso's 1946 diary. One page, matted with foam core, framed. 3000.
Abbey's typed ms. of an unfinished work, Sourdough Wilderness, c. 1954, make offer.

Leo was ready to rip. I couldn't see any reason to move. Wasn't that what got me in the first place?

"All right folks settle down.
In the southwest and all over Indian country people have lots of song about coyote.

This one is a combination of several traditions.

The songs are supposed to have simple meanings like morality plays where the human is translated in animal terms.

I've taken to acting parts of it, so just hold still during the impersonations."

"One of the oldest tales among the White Mountain Apache is of a contest where the animals in high country at the beginning of October, when it begins to get cold, see who gets the title of best song of the year.

This year the finals were between coyote and elk.

All the other contestants were in the audience.

They gathered round the sacred Rock to see who would sing the best."

"Iisaw, the Hopi name of coyote, got first call."

Leo got down on his hands and knees, put his "paws" on the table surface of a rock beside him and tilted his head back like he was going to howl.

He had put on a costume too, a skin with a head like somebody's lost rug.

His mouth was open.

Saliva dripped off his tongue.

Words blended into cries and moans.

Like a coyote speaking English and a rooster starting to crow all at the same time.

Then he spun around a couple of times.

Everybody's in a daze.

The fire's throwing shadows off faces.

One minute it's like he disappeared, then the next he's back in a new costume.

Branches come out his collar and go up over his head.

It sounded like yips and caterwauls.

He's stuck his neck way out now, shakes his head back and forth.

The dudes have their mouths open.

He stretches his arms out with his head and lets out a long whistling cry.

So that's the way it was.

Leo blasted them into space.

This Meing, Mooing, Mewingmuling Song

> *Mule Fat (Baccharis salicifolia), Paphlagonian Sing along, a Canterbury pilgrimage of mules*

You expect mules to sing yo, hee, ho, like dwarves or Nibelungs, not be the souls of swing. But when next at a light you hear some chap talk, or he has the radio on, it's not that your blue-eyed Jack and Helen look like cars, they're mules of telecom.

"Ah guess you come here Lem to run the bottom," Harvey sang out the window to his astronautic Pole.

"But what is your text about the bare tomato, friend?"

The mules were telepathic.
"Profanation of a pig," thought Lem.
"Not what is but ought. First the tomato,
but a ham too big gets our leader shot."

Maybe we heard this once in translation, but no longer commune.

Lem denied.
"Yarvey, I seen a violet chigger."

He pledged to Helen sidelong; Helen frisked up her socks.

"Verst vessel, I will scoot thy hinny bottom."

Lem harrumphed, but not in song.

Mule speech is a version of ancient tongue known to prospectors
with spades and boots.
They muck about fresh language universals, in other words, make
mule thought a man's.

What's wrong with man that he thought his thought gone wrong?
That effort engendered all this meing, mooing, mewingmuling song.

The mules shared their feelings.
"Why can't a car salesman tie his shoe?" called Mervin, the
aforementioned ham.
"Cause he's worried you will too!"

Harvey replied:

"What happened when a car salesman opened the door?"
They all joined in. "Harfs from the front, haws from the rear."
 "The serial numbers escaped."
"He lost his tassels."

It was a scene from the social classes.

Then in order:

"My oh my what a wonder bonjeur"
"I got a feel-ing!"
"Wun-der-ful feel-ing!"
"Oh the warmth of a honky's ass."

Mervin, lead chorister, again led out:

"On Doppel, on Schussel."

Others followed suit:

"*On hind end die blumen.*"
 "Ass on Boddle."

"Bestrudal mine bier kanne."

They were just horsing around.
Man calls him mulish, but mules know those plans to terra-form
planets.
They know the man lost his life in his own garden when his ear pod
jammed.
Bionic ears for labyrinthitis didn't make him hear.

Where had all the bodies gone?
He still doesn't know.
The man of sin rode his back.
The mules knew that.
They called to it in scat.

"Om Dancer, om Prancer,
be smirchen sie hovel...."

The mules themselves thought that the world was reversed.
That mules could talk but riders were mute.
Molecules murmured. Croton was alive, but not in cars.

There was still just the one man around as before.
You could tell by his spore. He talked on his cell.

In mule code the man with earplug and blindfold believed he could
hear,
but the mule believer rode bare.

Each comedic phone took a turn.

"Curb the beast in a man and will you find a mule? A dog? A pony?"

"Shall we play Old Donny?"

"Do mules play Beethoven?"

The chorus hustled:
"And in this mule we found an ape.

Eee haw, eee haw, oh.
And in that ape we found a duck.
And a holy cow.
With a swineherd here and a swineherd there…"

They pantomimed ape routines from late night TV of his fears.

"We want our flesh but we don't want theirs!
"Think of all the disgusting hairs."
"Red Rob! It's not the flesh I hate."
"It's the indigestion of the pate."

"Oh, cover yourself."
"We fill the God hole with ourselves."
"There is a god for these hands and hearts, *volks esse*."

This parson mule was so sage he looked like a horse.

So is the beast in a mule manmade like in a car?

Different versions of this quandary occur.
A man blames his body. A medical condition.
The more versions he has the more dangerous, because after them,
liberty falls and periodicity comes in doubt.
Equanimity's down like a lightening bug.
Hyperspace landings at the Pentagon were sold.

Chronics complain: "we can't see it, we can't feel it, how do you
know it's there?"
They forgot what they were, wanted to make cabbalistic payments
for the conflict of flesh until death.

In the aftermath of this humorous wedding of the head
antiphony pricked the soft hearted aloe first, then truth.
The mules had long since learned to sing what a man could hardly
speak, but reversed.

It was out on the rest stop, hot and cool, when the dialectics began.

"Squirt the hose for wetness."
"Kick a tire in the leg."
"How do you know you're not just imagining?"
"Evil asks, 'Is there good?'"

But there is one thing about the mule spirit. It negotiates from the heart. These mules appointed their answers out of rock. Gaseous Garvey, Red Rob, Hickey, vied throughout.

All were Pegasusians.

We reproduce an audio portion for the internationale pod mind that cannot hear.
Or you may strap a wireless on the tail.

Savor if you will.
It crested toward the feet of tourists making their way dialectically past,
but wearing only sandals.

We dare not translate this *strudal vagen* speech.

The mules were swearing.

Freeze the frame at the apogee of sense, the mule river running, asteroids fallen, but holding their breath at the stench.
How long can a mule hold its breath?

Voices broadcast off canyon walls. Even the last in line could hear the dilemmas that think they are our last thoughts before going to bed.

The drip drop of mule feet, leaking canteens, stumbling feet, red dust black streaks on limestone, red shale, white cliffs. The switchbacks plop plop the feet, clip clop, plop plop, drip drop, the canteens leak. Ground squirrels at the feet, some kid whistles at a moth.

"That's a nice spot they found there."

"I see people up there."
A borderline of trees and rocks, then I see the top. Then just single trees, trees, trees. Then the sky-perfect blue.
The print of boots lap and overlap.
"I want a drink please – in what language that you?"
"You're standing on my big box kite"
"Let's make another."
"We'll get a stone and draw something. What you making TiTi?"
"A big box kite with six eyes.'
Now let's 'stroy it!"
"Four strings, and the cheeks!"
People have to be holding it.
What people?
The people I'm making.
Make the heads and the face and the nose.
They need a penis!
No, they're girls.
Do mans' have penises? Make a man.
No, they're all women and girls.
She holding that kite?

Brown mules dragged the tip the back hoof. Dingy whites, sorrels, the blacks no better pass. Thigh muscles cramp by the time the mules stop, plop, the mule changes feet. Hordes pass hatless, shirtless to be red skinned.

They think what they speak, but they speak what they hear.
A little Virgil, misunderstood Spanish, mused pidgin, English and Japanese.
It's not the grammar of the OED or the cable hop of soaps that carouses the mind.
This crew had just carted a company of Volkswagens, those engaged with the Faust. Which led to the ultimate question:

"You mean there is conflict with the physical body?"
 "It's a Mcdonald's without the meat!"
 "A spiritual burger has spiritual meat?"
"There's no monkey wrench without a monkey!"

Reasserting his mutter-sprach quest for meaning, Mervin dissertated
man in his passion:

"But Johnny Cake outran every other.
Johnny Cake,
Pan Cake
Hip like law
outran his brothers
the wolf and the bear."

Then all the brothers joined in.

"They visited Darwin , but fell on a stone."
"Fox waited in spirit, hoodwinked the bone."
"Sly as a coyote, that one fox, dangerous as wolf."
 "Friendly like a dog and prettier than all."

Crescendo: "thump, thump, thump, the animals come."

There had been talk all that day about the image reversed of raven
and owl that hid in the buyer's intestate brain when he indulged his
emotions, which fear provoked the impulse to buy.
They graphed this on an upward sloping line.
But there was no cooling off period.
These mules knew the high and the low.
They had the mo.
Johnny was their image of man.

"But spiritually another case, Johnny stuffed with cotton. His shoe
eyes were buttoned,
The little rag spirit and loppy head were empty and hollow in bed."

Cap had a coda:
"You could use corn shucks and wadding!"

It's as likely to hear of the rose from a wasp in the garden
as it is to hear from the mule on high trail.
Or the hawk overhead, the eagle clothed trees,
the walnut wonder of everything that breathes.

Do salesmen raise their hands and heads?
By now the mules were texting:

"There used to be an outer, there used to be an in."
"There's a spiritual organ in circumcision."
"*Die dicke ende.*"
"Once circumcised, the truth is out."
"It's the fleshy heart of plaque, not yarrow stalks."

You can say mules don't talk, don't text, that the new car doesn't
smell, that they didn't say that or that nobody could hear.

Solipsism becomes the man of dust.
Caroling washes him off.

Speech will undo deafness.
The elk, the raven, the mule song and the bear.
Everything that has breath praises.

But atoms kidded the man.

The mules were edgy to ride.

"Cut, then cover."
"Cut the fat."
"You can't take back the sac."
"Clothe the heart."
"I buy the rack."

"What do you think the salesman sold tonight?
Want to take it home and show it to the wife?"

In the landing was the takeoff.
Seatbelts everyone.
Fasten your trays.
The captain is about to depart.
Upright if you please.

"Spiritual worlds ruin the physical."
"You think good is evil and evil is good?"
"The boy in the hood, the cow that could, dead meat for food?"
"Be schmutzen der esel."
A mule shook a hoof.

"Stay higher mind. Stay, stay put."
"A brick of a burger in spiritual speak."
"A burger will satisfy, not spiritual rock."
"What if the end comes and I don't think?"
We can get too much of this stuff.

Time was it was excellent to just say goodbye.
As all tourists in the astonished trail, by prearranged signal the fresh
mules mount. pushed out.

Mervin with praise breath, bellowed the wonder-sprach, "espiritu
speak."

What a Dog Coyote Sings AI-AI-OO-OO and Other Visions of Iisaw

The Indians call me Walto Dog. *Walto-Dog. What-A-Dog!* I sing
myself and shake the hills. Stop this night with me and loose your
throat.

> Once a time in fairy tale
> a dog would save the *pekldfille*.
> Man he was all loving the *pep0le*.
> Oh he went saving the *peoopel*.
> In alleys, down basements, protect,
> *pertect, peertect du peoplez*."

But I don't like da doggie.

Ya-honk.
Do not compare me to doggie.
I don't like *peple. Pepel.* Ya' think?

Donot

compare

me to

pepel

What am I, a sign of democracy? Nobody likes *peo;le.* That pahana
peonist, Porky Borg, he come over you better pull out you sock.
Better a door prize than a berm of dirt. Jacky Doodle. DOGGY DAY
LILY

What'll it be today mum? Some tiger?"
"Slice me up the heart dear."
The *pleoplle* always the *ploody pop-ple.*

Coyot,
wog,
peonist,
dog.

Every atom belonging to you belongs to me.
Remember all the nasty bait.

Down down doggy burrowed in the dirt, shot from plane!
By daffo-dog down burrowed and broiling fresh game.
Wulfs? I used to have books.
Like Lish did Carver, a peonist prom,
Walk a mile in my brudder don't mean wear him out the store.
I walk them holes with dogs and wolves.

Exterminate the rattlesank, pigens and oh, *ya tried true* stuff.
Uh huh, ya tried.
They seeks you here they seeks you there,
Little Tommy Tucker's dog, man they shot him down.
Doom down.
Man in the moon down.
Dogologist in wood, lover with fat pud, he down.
What'd ye say brethren? Every atom belonging to you belongs to me.

"Two for one.
Eat for Fun.
Join the corp
with Strum und Drang."

"I will use you tenderly," ♫ sings my supper and its Franklin mind.
♫
That franker. He down this season.
We all gonna be one Franklin!
A few light kisses and we all gonna be *one Franklin till the buzzard come.*
Grind on, grind on, don't make me prowl old campsites snooting cans.
Undrape! Undrape! What you assume I shall.
Mystically nude, out of the dimness I sing myself.
What's an idea dressed up as a meal? I had him next me at table, Bill.
Outlaw, I loafe, invite my soul. Have a blade of grass. OOOO!
A beverage and some treats. Diddle down them animals.
The two are one. Drink and eat. I see that as a law. On one you eat,
but on two, what's a meal but a pie hopin' to work? The perp!
Coyotes meet in dormer, somebody gets hurt.
Bloody necks, bloody toes, hankering, gross.

AI-AI-OOOO! Blood flows.

This the gloam of coyote talk. We sing so why not talk? and if talk why not wait and write the unacknowledged verse? Indians call me *Walt-A-Dog*. I shake myself and sing.

From the river like a snooting can the rim sticks up. What's in it? Screeches, caves, trees, the same frustrations in canyons and on plains, not enough food. I was waiting when Gravel, Trump, a body rolled up. You order out? Delivery? Sauce? What won't come to one who waits? It was getting close to dark.

Knowing The Terrible, a tourist, fell from the Rim. Search parties were mounted, but had to be mounted again. He lay out the night predation.

The dust cleared. There sat an alpine hat with the bristle gone. And Swiss jodhpurs. Made me want to yodel, which you know is beautiful. Braised and beautiful without the bun. Take what comes. Strum and Drang. The roll? Mid age. Tender. Ready. I am putting on a napkin when my meal spoke.

Help, it said, help me, I fell.

Attn: Anaxagoras, Empedocles. This guy blind? Don't he yote? His eyes were full of dirt and swoll. He couldn't smell. They lost that. Didn't know I could talk. Played a trick, being bored. I said in my Best Western voice, "help is coming, just rest and let me look at that leg." I went over to lick the blood.

He said, *that feels good, what's your name.*

When *the man* asks you your name and he don't hear so good this is what you say. "*Amo-le, from the Nahuatl.*" You know. A yucca to make you pucka. Talk about the luck, he was a literary agent! and me unpublished and all. Like he was a tour guide wrapped in one who wandered and fell down. In shock it began to talk, had repped Updike once and knew the New Yap strip poets. Wee tricksy there, but to entertain him with my poetic song, which he said he would be glad to hear, for we had *the long night when no man can work.* Talked funny. I executed my sequence on Not Being food. Close to the heart. Took some practice arpeggios and sailed in three quarter time.

I am a Samaritan of the cold. Bloody necks, bloody toes, hankering

AI- AI-OOOO! blood flows.

The name comes from Watha, to quote the venerable Iisaw!

> "He ate the corn,
> He ate the fawn,"
> he slay the bone,
> coyotes complain.

Take a breath and let it out. That's what I'm talkin' 'bout. Heal my pain oh gob'ment! Oh inaprecio lastma!

The guy made no peep so I stopped. What ya think, he dead?

"Hey it reminds of those renaissance plays of Marston and Bruno, a kind black eye in the hole of lit. Do much misanthrope and the little presses will have a go. We have a piece about a guy who eats the universe. Piper sing that song again that merry pipe. Is there a second verse?"

So I piped my song to hear.

♪
I loved blood more than berry and beetle,
I loosed blood more than Arthropod.
I've no mouse in store for a tiny carcass, a wish for a centipede.
I seek the lame, halt and blind in my way, for impurity lives.
I'm a doctor, a healer. There to help I came, to introduce painless to pain.

You feel pain, scatter teeth, rename. Hiawatha What-A-Dog!.
I be down to get you in the broadcloth shrubbery.

I see through the honey.
 Hiawatha! Medium of change and exchange that forgives.
All pass but this, the blood that washes, commerce of the same. ♪

**Take my comrade Clumsy Oaf who fell out the shelf. He
delivered from a hole in the box and he bust.**

♫ And now the warm white bread I eat.
Hig a pig a pop.
wants a helicopter take out.
I show up.

Polly put the kettle on
this jug so empty,
and serve my frien.'
Loaf on the grass,
agued pie of my fast.

The best of the toothsome fat is the blab of the pave.
Folks who do damage, do the meal. ♫

He again: *It has a nice naturalistic flair to it with the oral repetition,
might have some appeal to the nature crowd.*

—As I was becoming believed, I said, let me try out for you
something I'm working on right now, It's called

Daffo-Dog

Yes, he said.
By then his eyes looked even worse, filmy orbs that distilled a rheum
and he began to cough.

How long have you had that cough, I asked.
It's nothing, he said.
I pretended to fuss over him then, conjured all sorts of remedies, but
he said, "Enough," the cough's a mere nothing; it will not kill me. I
shall not die of a cough. Sing some more, it helps kill the time."

So yet once more ye laurels and ye myrtles brown with ivy sere I come to pluck your berries harsh and crude.

Daffo-Dog

A was for the apple.
I cut it for food.
B was for the baby bird I visit after school.
We ate the hot fry.
D, when day was over, I could see the moon.
But my Binky could not rise.
Rise up you stars of stew.
I flown down a brandy,
a ruff-cask pooch with stuff.
Diddle down them animals,
Iron or ivory, with the nerve to call.
We get to know each other.
I am poet of Body and Soul. ***What-A-Dog Cosmos!***

Can you speak?
That lantern make you flit.
We both got to fend for life and truth. I did.
My tongue, every atom of blood
Form'd from this soil, this air,
Poet of Body and Soul,
Born of parents there. Creeds in abeyance
I harbor a school.
Long that smile I feasted. ***What-A-Dog Cosmos!***

Night was getting on by then. Entrainment evening faded like a ether bubble. Not that I was out of song, oh no, the word hoard glittered with raw jewel, beef in a deli, if you catch my flight. But the ruse was getting slight.

Long that mile I feasted I did. I said.
He groaned.
You speak? I said.

He had lit a lantern. "That lantern make you flit."
"We have gotten to know each other." I said

"My tongue, every atom of blood form'd from this soil, this air, poet of Body and Soul, born of parents here and there, held creeds in abeyance." I said, thinking of my lost chalice of evening, "I harbor a school of mice. Is it not fair that this exchange be consummated?"

Unknowing, terrible,
the tourist fell from Rim.
Down, down, down,
Down bedubby down
Search parties pronounced
had to be mounted again."

He starts to applaud. "*Wonderful*," he says, "*a real flair for the unconscious. That name in there ai ai oo. I sounds like the cry of a coyote. I believe that could be something.*"

The name derives from Watha, I said, to quote what liver Iisaw said:

3.

When you go to defeat your enemy
hang him round your neck like a bowling ball.
Make him into a god, hang his head inside,
put him on your wrist for life insurance.
Sell him to tourists. They need more gods.

Speak Space Voyager from the mountain side.
♫ "I'll be down to get cha in a broadcloth honey.
You better be ready so I won't be late,
you one nice dry pig. ♫

"There's nothin' you can do 'cept age and wait."

That's what I bin doin' Momma, waitin,' talking like a fairy poem.
Momma Noture, I got dandelion. I got hair.

Wait.
ya dirty moth.
You ate a year.

Momma stopped by the kettle store. Weverboy's been walking round
with nuts inside.
Weverboy's on a first name basis with a nut, he burn you like
Holland then he rests.

You want a good hound?
I wear a hood of grey.

Gold locks, red locks,
black locks down,
Top-knot to love-cur
The hair wisps down.

A merry pumpkin said to me: I'm plumpkin and you were too. But
he din't.
In the heart the button holds ordain the patterned world.

Mal-wole! **Oh, oh.**

Why oh why oh why-o,
Why oh why oh why?
Because, because, because, because
Goodbye, goodbye, goodbye.

"How extract the strength from beef? Every atom belonging to you
belongs to me."
If you need savin' wouldn't you bring a horse?"

"My guide took sick Jack, jack he did, he died and now I'm waitin."

*"But they told me you packed dudes in the states, that you know the
country from Cheops to Tuklate. We planned three nights on the trail
so I got provisions."*

"Do not lick the face, son."

Momma! I know something. Course that is to tell.
One time I bit some hormone dame with <u>tricksy breath</u>. Civilization
took a poll to find out who would press the beast!
It shall be you!

"I been down river, but never leading a cry..."

"Oh well don't worry about that son, I'm the leader!"

www.ingramcontent.com/pod-product-compliance
Lightning Source LLC
Chambersburg PA
CBHW070933130626
46555CB00001B/414